Traitor's Game

Rosemary Hayes

For Joyce,
with very best
wishes,
Rosemary

Rosemary Hayes
2024

First published in 2024 by Sharpe Books.

Chapter One

October 1808

'Bastard!'

Sergeant Armstrong shifted himself up into a sitting position on the deck of the barge.

'Bastard,' he muttered again, looking up at Will Fraser, until recently Captain of the Highland Light Infantry, who stood beside him, legs braced against the slurp of the tide, staring down at the grey waters of the River Thames.

Will Fraser dragged his thoughts back to the present. The privations and disgrace of the preceding weeks had taken their toll. His face was pale and drawn but he managed a faint smile.

'Addressing me, Sergeant?' he asked.

Armstrong shook his head and rubbed at the stump of his arm. 'You know who I mean Captain, I …'

Will sighed. 'Don't call me Captain.'

'Can't help it sir.'

'Or sir. I'm not an officer.'

'Are to me sir, always will be.'

Will squatted down beside the Sergeant. 'How's the arm?'

'Gone,' said Armstrong, glad to see another brief smile cross Fraser's face. 'Och, it's not so bad,' he went on. 'I feel a deal better now we're off that stinking ship.'

The hospital ship bringing the wounded back from Portugal had been a leaky vessel with a belligerent crew. They'd had a miserable voyage.

Soldiers were used to dry land beneath their feet; most of the wounded on the ship had suffered terrible seasickness and many had died on the voyage. And those men still strong enough to voice their opinions had spent what energy they possessed hurling insults at the French prisoners of war sharing the cramped conditions on board.

The vessel had been storm tossed in the Bay of Biscay and further delayed by contrary winds until, at last, it had limped into the Channel and the wounded taken off the ship at Spithead.

After more delay, Fraser and Armstrong, with the rest of the wounded bound for London, had been transferred to one of the large estuary barges. Now that the tide was in they were finally making their way up the River Thames.

Their barge was one of many moving up and down the great river, all sailing low in the water, though theirs carried broken men, not the normal cargo of hay, rubbish, sand, grain or gunpowder.

Will Fraser, however, was not one of these broken men - at least not in body. He had no physical wounds.

Small knots of people gathered on the shore and stopped what they were doing to stare at the barge, the keen-eyed spotting the soldiers' uniforms. At one place there was quite a large number of folk and they began cheering as the barge sailed past, but none of the men on board responded.

Will looked across at the excited crowd. 'No doubt they'll have read the dispatches about the great victory at Vimeiro and the glory of Sir Arthur Wellesley,' he said bitterly.

'No doubt sir,' said Armstrong.

But neither man was thinking of that great victory. Their thoughts were of escape from death, of a rescue condemned as cowardice, and of jealousy and betrayal.

As they sailed further towards the city, the traffic increased and there was much activity along the river. New docks were under construction and trading vessels were loading and unloading their cargoes.

Will Fraser and Duncan Armstrong were from the North of England but there were other soldiers on board more familiar with London.

'There's been a good deal of construction these past years,' said one of them. 'The new East India docks do a brisk business.'

Aye,' said another. 'When our ships blockaded the French ports, Bonaparte told his allies to stop trading with Britain, but it's made no difference to trade with the East.'

After they passed Wapping wharf, the river became ever more congested. Will shouted to one of the four crew members who were skilfully steering the barge out of the way of other boats. 'When shall we be set ashore?'

The man shouted back, over his shoulder. 'We'll tie up this side of Blackfriars Bridge, near St Paul's,' he said.

At last the crew lowered the sails, manoeuvred the vessel towards the river's edge and after a lot of shouting and cursing, managed to find a space to tie up.

Armstrong and Fraser watched as some of the more badly wounded men were taken off and loaded onto carts.

The walking wounded gathered by the edge of the water to say their farewells before dispersing, some in groups of two or three, some singly. Now that they were no longer travelling along the water, the stench of the river was more obvious.

'You'll be going to your brother's lodgings, will you sir?' asked Armstrong.

Will nodded. He looked up at the dull October sky which was already beginning to darken. 'It's a good step from here. I should be on my way.'

He picked up his haversack and slung it over his shoulder. 'And you, Sergeant? You mentioned an inn where you could lodge.'

Armstrong nodded at a group of departing soldiers. 'They told me of the Haycart in Seven Dials,' he said. 'Cheap and not too flea-ridden, by all accounts.'

'We'll walk together then. My brother lodges in Drury Lane.'

Will offered to take Armstrong's haversack, but only received a snarl of refusal in reply.

As they made their way along the river's edge, past the great Cathedral of St Paul's on their right, they had to share the street with carriages bowling along and a variety of wagons and carts transporting goods. When at length, they turned away from the river and then West down Fleet Street, the traffic was even heavier, folk heading for their homes or out to seek entertainment, and several times they were shouted at and told to make way.

When they reached Drury Lane, and the address of Will's brother, the two men stopped. Unthinking, Will held out his right hand to the Sergeant.

'Nothing to shake that side,' said Armstrong. He put his haversack down on the ground and held out his left hand. 'Try this one.'

They stood side by side for a few moments, hands clasped. Armstrong began to speak but Will stopped him. 'Too much to say, Sergeant,' he muttered.

'Aye,' said Armstrong. Then he picked up his haversack and, without a backward glance, strode off in the direction of Seven Dials.

Will watched him until he turned a corner and was out of sight then he shut his eyes and for a moment relived that fateful moment which had ended his career.

If I had my time again, would I have acted differently?

But he knew that, despite everything, he would not - could not - have done so. He swallowed, braced his shoulders and banged on the door in front of him. It would be good to see his brother again.

Pray God that Jack will understand.

There was no response so, after a few minutes he banged again, more forcefully this time, and at last heard the sound of shuffling feet and some muttering from within. Then the door was opened a crack and a woman's head appeared. She looked Will up and down.

'Yes?'

Will smiled. 'I'm Jack Fraser's brother, Madame. Will Fraser, at your service. Is my brother in?'

The woman came out to stand in the doorway. She was of middle years, neatly dressed and with strong, knowing features. She folded her arms and stared at him.

Slightly discomforted, Will cleared his throat. 'He will want to see me,' he said.

She frowned. 'He's not here.'

Will's shoulders drooped and he was suddenly overwhelmed with fatigue. The weariness and despair he had been fighting against these last weeks returned with a force that almost made him stagger.

I have been staking all on this reunion.

He took a deep breath. 'Madame, I have had a long journey. May I come in and wait for him?'

She frowned. 'I told you, sir, he is not here. He's gone.'

'Gone,' said Will, unable to understand her meaning. 'Gone where?'

She shrugged. 'No idea. There've been others looking for him.' Then she came a little closer. 'You certainly resemble him, though. I can believe you're his brother.'

Will was tempted to snap at her, but he restrained himself. 'When was he last here?'

'A week ago. I've not seen hide nor hair of him since.'

'And his belongings?'

'All gone. Cleared out and vanished. Never gave me notice.'

Will looked over his shoulder. It was nearly dark now and Drury Lane was not well lit. He possessed no means of defending himself in these unfamiliar London streets should he lose his way or fall among thieves. He turned back to the woman.

'Is my brother's room vacant, Madame?'

'You wish to rent it?'

'It is getting late, Madame. I would be much obliged.'

She only hesitated for a moment before nodding and opening the door for him.

Jack will have paid her until the month's end, I'm sure of it. She sees a way of making extra coin.

The woman was all smiles now, introducing herself to him as Mrs Baxter, showing him round, indicating where he could wash and asking if he would like her to serve him some victuals.

'You have the bearing of a military man, sir,' she said. 'Have you returned from overseas?'

Will nodded but did not elaborate.

'Which regiment, if I may ask?'

'I am no longer a soldier, Madame,' he said.

The words still pained him. He cleared his throat. 'Will you be so good as to show me to my brother's room.'

The ceilings were low and Will had to stoop to avoid cracking his head on the stout beams, but the house was clean and well appointed.

'Have you other lodgers?' he asked, as he followed Mrs Baxter through the main room and towards the staircase.

She nodded. 'A laundress and her husband and child in the back bedroom,' she said, pointing down a passage, 'then two young actresses in the attic.' She sighed. 'The poor lasses were booked for a season at the Theatre Royal in Covent Garden, but then the building burnt down last month.'

'How unfortunate,' said Will, sensing that a response was expected.

'Unfortunate indeed if they cannot pay me,' she muttered.

Mrs Baxter led him up the narrow wooden stairs to the landing and opened a door on the right. Inside, the room was spacious and plainly furnished and as Will glanced around, he imagined Jack inhabiting it, his garments strewn carelessly over the chair and his boots under the bed. There was nothing, though, to indicate that the room had been recently occupied, not a whiff of Jack's presence.

'For how long will you wish to take the room?'

Will heaved his haversack off his back and put it on the bed. 'Only for tonight.'

Mrs Baxter made no comment but her smile vanished and she glanced down at his worn boots.

She knows I must seek cheaper lodgings than this.

He handed over some of his dwindling supply of coin to cover the cost of the room and his food. Mrs Baxter counted it out carefully then put it into the pocket of her dress.

She sniffed. 'This is my best room,' she remarked as she turned to go down the stairs. 'Your brother was very satisfied with it.'

When she had left, Will took off his short-fronted tailcoat and hung it over a chair, then he thoroughly inspected the room. He looked under the bed, in the wardrobe and lifted the lid of the desk which stood beneath the window. He opened every one of its drawers but found nothing. At length, he lay stretched out on the bed and laced his hands behind his head.

What happened, Jack? Why did you leave with such haste? Where have you gone?

His eyes began to droop and although he was mortally tired, he resisted the urge to let his body relax into sleep and at length hauled himself to his feet and went in search of victuals and the pump in the yard.

Mrs Baxter had laid out some food for him in the small parlour at the back of the house – a loaf of bread, some cooked meats, anchovies, hard-boiled eggs and onions. Will was ravenous and fell upon the victuals as if this were the last time he'd be well fed.

Which it may well be.

A young servant girl appeared with a jug of ale. She blushed as she set it down beside the food and made to scuttle away but Will stopped her.

'What is your name?'

The girl bobbed a slight curtsy, her eyes on the floor. 'Betsy, sir,' she whispered.

Will smiled at her. 'I'm Jack Fraser's brother, Betsy,' he said.

She nodded. 'Mrs Baxter said.'

'Do you have any notion where he's gone?'

She shook her head.

'Did he have visitors while he was here?'

She nodded. 'Some men sir.'

'Do you remember their names?'

She shook her head again.

'Were they old men or young?'

Betsy shrugged. 'Just men, sir. They came to see him most days.' She hesitated. 'They've been here since he left. They're mighty anxious to find him.'

'As am I, muttered Will.

There was a shout from the passage and Betsy turned to go, but at the door, she looked back.

'And a woman was here yesterday looking for him.'

'A woman?'

'She said she was his wife.'

Betty closed the door and Will stared after her.

His wife! Jack has no wife!

Back in his room, Will took off his long boots and inspected them. They were mud stained and down at heel but they would have to suffice. He wiped them down carefully then reached into his haversack for some blacking and rubbed the mixture into the leather. He took off his waistcoat and pantaloons and put them over the chair with his topcoat. They were the only civilian garments he possessed. When he'd been stripped of his uniform and his rank, he'd had to wear them constantly since he left Portugal. They were travel worn and stained, but he had no others. Will sat on the edge of his bed, his head in his hands, then finally, overcome with exhaustion, he lay down and fell asleep.

For some time he slept soundly but in the hours just before dawn he woke from a nightmare, reliving his humiliation and shouting out in exasperation. Gradually, he surfaced and looked about him, confused, at first, by his surroundings until the events of the previous day came back to him. He couldn't sleep any longer, turning round in his mind what he must do. His predicament was dire. He had little money and no contacts in London save Jack. He had to find him.

Chapter Two

At length, Will abandoned any hope of sleep and crept down the stairs and out into the yard to use the privy. On his way in again he almost collided with a young woman cradling a mewling infant in her arms.

She started when she saw him. 'Oh sir, you're back. We've been that worried …' Then she stopped and frowned, looking at him more carefully.

Will smiled. 'I'm Mr Fraser's brother Madame. Will Fraser, at your service.'

'Forgive me sir. In this light I thought …'

The baby started yelling once more and the woman hoisted it over her shoulder and patted its back.

Will made way for her to pass but then remembered what Mrs Baxter had said.

'Are you the laundress, Madame?'

She nodded, glancing at his filthy shirt and pantaloons which he'd donned again for decency. 'I can launder those for you if you wish, sir.'

Will nodded. 'I am ashamed to give them to you in this state, but I have no other clothes … and little coin,' he added under his breath.

'Wait here,' she said, disappearing into the back bedroom with the baby and emerging, a few minutes later, with some clean clothes.

'Here sir, these are my husband's,' she said. 'Put them on and leave your soiled linen at my door. I can have them laundered by evening.'

As the woman and baby went into the yard to get water, Will quickly stripped in the passage and donned the garments.

Never have I appreciated clean linen more.

Back in his room, he brushed down his waistcoat and topcoat and tried to make a plan.

But every plan involved finding Jack.

At length, he went down to the small parlour in search of victuals and found Mrs Baxter in urgent conversation with two young women he assumed were the actresses she'd mentioned who lived in the attic. Their voices were raised, Mrs Baxter's voice the loudest.

'You know the rules. A month's rent in advance. Due tomorrow; if it's is not paid by the end of the week you go elsewhere.'

'But you know our situation! It's not our fault the theatre burnt down. We'll find something soon. Pray be patient. Give us a little more time I beg you.'

'Huh! Patience. Patience won't put food on the table. I run a lodging house, not a charity. A month's rent by Friday or you pack your bags.'

The conversation died as Will entered the room. He cleared his throat. 'Good morning ladies.'

Three pairs of eyes turned towards him. Both young women gasped but Mrs Baxter immediately apprised the girls of the situation.

'Sally, Lottie, this is Mr Will Fraser. Mr Jack's brother.'

Sally giggled and bobbed a curtsy. 'We can see that,' she said. 'Why, at first I thought Mr Jack had returned.'

Mrs Baxter raised her eyes to the ceiling then, calling to Betsy to bring some food, she left the room.

Will found the girls' company refreshing and as the three of them ate their breakfast of bread and porridge, Sally and Lottie kept him entertained with their lively chatter.

'We were offered a Winter season at the Royal,' said Lottie, 'Then the theatre only bloody went and burnt down.'

'If we want regular work we'd have to join a company,' said Sally, 'But if you do that they expect you to be a frow - and we're not going down that road.'

Will had been among soldiers long enough to know what frow meant.

'We had plenty of work in the summer,' Sally went on. 'There were pageants and plays and tableaux and all sorts. But now there's not even work in Vauxhall Gardens.' She sighed. 'We'll have to move out of here. Ma Baxter won't keep us if we can't pay.'

Lottie broke off a chunk of bread and put it in her pocket. 'Truth to tell, I'll not be sorry. She was all smiles when we were earning but now we're out of work, she's that sour.'

'Where will you go?' asked Will.

Lottie shrugged and glanced at Sally. 'We'll just have to doss down with some of the other girls 'til we can find a place.'

'I'll be moving on today, too,' said Will.

The girls stared at him.

Should I tell them that I'm a disgraced soldier with no money?

'I have to find my brother,' he said simply. 'And … and I need to find cheaper lodgings, too.'

Sally recovered first. 'But you're a gentleman.'

Will smiled. 'Not much of a gentleman now, Sally. I have little coin and no income.'

'Where will you go?' asked Lottie.

'I heard there's cheap lodging in Seven Dials, at the Haycart.'

The girls exchanged looks.

'Do you know of it?' asked Will.

'I should say so,' said Sally. 'Seven Dials is the worst rookery in town. And they say the Haycart's a flash tavern.'

'Flash?'

'Criminals. The Haycart's where they drink, the thieves and suchlike.'

Will frowned. 'I think my Sergeant - my friend,' he corrected himself. 'I think he has gone there and I thought to seek him out.'

Sally and Lottie said nothing.

Will arranged to leave his haversack with Mrs Baxter and return later to fetch it and collect his laundered clothes, then he donned his topcoat and made for the door. Sally and Lottie were making ready to leave, too.

'You be sure to take care sir,' said Lottie.

Will turned back to smile at them. 'I can look after myself.'

As he stepped out into Drury Lane, his mood was matched by the leaden sky. The rain had ceased but the streets were wet and slippery from a recent shower. The smog from the chimneys belching thick smoke made his eyes smart and the crowds gave him no quarter, pushing and shoving, carts loaded with goods of all sorts pulled by skinny horses and men driving cattle to the slaughterhouses in the East of the capital. Will had to keep stepping aside to avoid the press of folk and the filth in the streets.

It was not a long walk to Monmouth Street in Seven Dials and he'd been given directions, but his mood did not lighten as he drew nearer and he began to understand the warnings he'd been given. Although there were shops - ironmongers, woodcarvers, straw hat manufacturers, pork butchers, watch repairers, wigmakers and booksellers - there were many public houses and slum dwellings, too, bursting with humanity of all sorts. As he fought his way through, he was constantly approached by beggars, folk selling ballads and political tracts, drunks and prostitutes and as he entered the Haycart public house, it was with a mixture of fear and relief.

The place was crowded but the moment he walked in, the room fell silent and all eyes turned on him. For a moment, he was at a loss and then, through the fog of tobacco smoke and the smell of ale, came a familiar voice.

'Captain Fraser, sir. Come and join us.'

Grinning broadly, Will pushed his way through to a table at the back of the room where Sergeant Armstrong had stood up, his good hand outstretched. Will grabbed it and found himself momentarily lost for words.

Armstrong urged Will to sit down and sent for a fresh jug of ale and in due course, conversation resumed around them with rough laughter, ribald comments and the unmistakeable aroma of unwashed bodies.

'What brings you here, sir?'

'Don't call me sir,' muttered Will, taking a long draught of ale. Then he proceeded to tell the Sergeant all that had happened in Drury Lane, of Jack's disappearance, of his mysterious visitors and so-called wife, and of his own precarious situation.

Armstrong listened in silence, nodding from time to time and when Will came to the end of his story, he frowned.

'Well, there's no lack of cheap lodging in Seven Dials, sir, but it's mighty crowded. This tavern's full to bursting but I've found a place a few doors down. It's cheap as dirt 'cos the journeymen sub-let and I'm sharing the one room with a couple and their three children and another returning soldier.'

Will tried not to look shocked and Armstrong laughed. 'It's a roof, sir – and it's better than dossing down on the deck of that hospital ship. Leastways, it'll do until my pension comes in.'

Will nodded. Had he not left the army in disgrace, he, too, would have had a pension.

'Doubtless we can find you something round here sir, just 'til you meet up with your brother, but it won't be what you're used to.'

'What I'm used to is dust and flies and army tents, as you very well know.'

They talked some more and Armstrong bought them a couple of pies, then they went out looking for a room. Will felt more at ease now that he had the Sergeant for company but he was shocked by the filth, the poverty and the violence he saw. Several times, a fight broke out among men, women yelled at them or at each other and beggars constantly propositioned passers-by.

Armstrong pointed at one man, a rude wooden crutch lying beside him, holding out a bowl for alms.

'He says he's a soldier wounded in the wars but when I questioned him about his regiment and who he served under, he had no answer.' Armstrong coughed and spat onto the road. 'There's plenty pretending to be wounded soldiers, the bastards.'

Will was about to reply when another fight broke out only a few yards from them and they quickened their pace to avoid it.

'It's not too bad now,' said Armstrong. 'But they say the Watch have a mighty job keeping any order at night.'

'I can imagine,' said Will.

It took a deal of time but eventually, with Armstrong's help, Will had found a room in one of the quieter streets. It was small and dingy and he had to share it with another two men, but it was certainly cheap. He secured it for a week, paying less than he would pay for a single night at Mrs Baxter's establishment.

'How are you going to set about finding your brother, sir?' asked Armstrong, as they parted, Will to go and fetch his things from Drury Lane and Armstrong to return to the Haycart.

Will frowned. 'In truth, I don't know Sergeant. I know nothing of his London friends.'

'What work does he do?'

Will shook his head. 'It seems strange to say that I don't know, but I was overseas when he came here from the North. I know him so well as a brother yet his life here is a mystery to me.'

'Would you like company in your search?'

Will looked at the Sergeant and smiled. 'You will be much occupied finding your own feet, Sergeant. You'll not want to bother yourself with my troubles.'

There was a beat of silence, then Armstrong cleared his throat. 'You forget, sir, that many of your troubles arose because of what you did for me. I am in your debt and I would like to repay you.' Then he grinned. 'Besides, you know I like an adventure!'

By the time Will neared Drury Lane, the sun was shining brightly and there was a light breeze clearing the smoke-filled air. His step became lighter as he walked towards Mrs Baxter's lodging house. His mood had lifted after seeing Armstrong and his thoughts turned to the time they had spent together in Portugal, of Armstrong's bravery and loyalty contrasting so sharply with the jealousy and skulduggery of the man who had caused Will's downfall.

Then his thoughts were interrupted by someone calling his name.

'Fraser!'

Will hesitated, frowning. No one knew him here. He began to turn towards the sound which came from an alley leading off the main street but then someone was suddenly beside him, grabbing him and dragging into the alley. Will tried to whip round to face his assailant but then another man was in front of him and before he had time to react further, he saw the dagger, the sun flashing briefly on its blade.

Will was no stranger to fighting but he had no weapon and he'd been taken by surprise. He shouted out but then immediately one of the men clamped a large hand over Will's mouth and the other raised his dagger to strike.

Chapter Three

Will twisted and kicked at the man above him and managed to unbalance him just enough so that the dagger missed its target at the first strike and plunged into Will's arm, but his assailant soon righted himself, pulled the dagger away and was readying to strike again while his companion pinned Will to the ground. Will bit the man's hand, kicked him in the groin so that he writhed on the ground in agony then he punched the other man's arm so that the dagger fell to the ground with a clatter and as the fellow bent to pick it up, Will snatched up the weapon and banged its blunt end onto the man's face with all the force he could muster. As he leapt free, one of the men lunged at his leg and only missed grabbing it by a matter of inches.

Clutching his injured arm, Will sprinted out of the alleyway and in moments was at Mrs Baxter's door, pounding on it with an urgency that brought Betsy running to look out of the window. Recognising Will, she made haste to unbolt the door. And when she saw the state of him her hand flew to her mouth.

'Why sir, whatever's happened? You are bleeding. Have you been attacked?'

For a few moments, Will stood beside her at the door breathing heavily, looking up and down the street. He caught sight of his attackers, whoever they were, staggering away as fast as they were able, and disappearing round the corner. He turned to Betsy.

'I'm sorry I frightened you, Betsy.'

Betsy's eyes were wide. 'You're bleeding sir,' she repeated. 'Come inside.'

In the hallway, Will looked down at his arm where blood was seeping right through to his topcoat. He took off his coat and rolled up his shirtsleeve. 'Perhaps you would be kind enough to fetch some water, Betsy, and some clean rags?'

She continued to stare at him.

'Now Betsy '

'Yes sir. Water and clean rags.'

She scuttled off but at the door she turned to look at him. Will smiled at her in what he hoped was a reassuring way though he was shaking. He knew that he had to apply pressure to the wound – and quickly. He was losing a lot of blood; the wound was deep and he was beginning to feel faint.

When the wound had been bound and the laundress prevailed upon to lend Will another shirt, he sat in the small parlour trying to collect his thoughts.

What in God's name was that all about? Those villains knew my name and would have murdered me. Did they mistake me for Jack? And if so, who is it that wishes him dead? No wonder he is lying low if he is in fear for his life.

He was not alone for long. Mrs Baxter bustled into the room, more concerned for the reputation of her lodging house than for Will's condition. She stood in front of him, her arms folded.

'I'll not have trouble brought to my door,' she announced. 'I'll be obliged if you would take your things and leave my house as soon as possible.'

'Madame, I …' began Will.

Mrs Baxter interrupted him. 'I can smell trouble,' she said, tapping her nose. 'And something stinks. First your brother ups and leaves without notice and his friends know nothing of his whereabouts. And now this.' She gestured at Will's arm. 'I'll warrant you were mistaken for your brother and he's in league with some wicked folk and in a deal of trouble.'

Will nodded. Much the same thought had occurred to him, but if that was the case then the Jack he knew – that young man of such charm and ability who had sacrificed much so that Will could buy his commission – that Jack had seemingly become a fugitive, running from those who wished to kill him. Will shook his head. He found it impossible to reconcile the two versions of the man.

His arm was throbbing and he felt weak but he knew he was no longer welcome.

'Madame. Give me a moment to collect my things and then I will be gone,' he said.

In truth, I do not relish the walk back to Seven Dials, but it is clear that I cannot stay here.

Mrs Baxter's next words mirrored his thoughts. 'Do not tarry.'

No compassion from that quarter. I'm trouble and she wants me gone.

Shakily, Will got to his feet and went to fetch his haversack. He collected his laundry and offered to pay for the ruined shirt but the young woman smiled at him. 'It turned out we had a good wash day in the end,' she said. 'The sun and wind dried the linen well this afternoon and I had made a fresh supply of soap last week. Your own clothes are dry and pressed and do not fret about the bloodied shirt, sir. The tear in it is easily mended and I'll soak it in lye and it'll come out good as new.'

Though it left him perilously short, Will gave the woman more coin than she demanded and wished her and her family well. As he was coming back through the house, Betsy forestalled him.

'There's a gentleman to see you in the parlour,' she said. 'Mrs Baxter's just let him in.'

Will frowned. He had no appetite for meeting more strangers.

'Who is he, Betsy?'

'I don't know his name sir, but he's a real gentleman. He's been here before to see Mr Jack. I think he's a friend of his.'

Will entered the parlour somewhat nervously, clutching his sore arm to his side and the man, who had been looking out of the window, his hands clasped behind his back, turned round to greet him.

'Ah, my good sir,' he said. 'Your landlady tells me Jack has not returned but that you are his brother. I am honoured to meet you. James Montagu, at your service.'

He extended his hand. Will took it and observed the man closely. If he was a friend of Jack's he was a new friend. Will was not acquainted with him.

The stranger was dressed in the latest fashion, wearing a close fitting dark blue wool cutaway tailcoat with a light-coloured waistcoat underneath, a white shirt and a spotless white linen cloth at his neck. His pantaloons were close fitting and his Hessian boots highly polished and sporting several tassels. His gloves, cane and beaver hat were placed on the table. Beside this elegant man about town, Will felt at a considerable disadvantage. His tussle with the ruffians in the alleyway had left his hair awry and his face smeared with dirt. And his arm throbbed horribly.

'May I know how you are acquainted with my brother, sir?'

Montagu hesitated and examined the back of his hand. 'We are colleagues, sir.'

'Colleagues?'

'Indeed. We both serve the Government.'

There was an uneasy silence while Will absorbed this information.

'Do you know where Jack is?' asked Will, at length. 'As you can imagine, I am anxious to find him.'

James Montagu sat down on one of the parlour chairs and crossed one elegant leg over the other. 'Alas, I do not.' He cleared his throat. 'Indeed, I had hoped that you might have news of him.' He looked up and, for the first time, met Will's eyes. 'I have to confess, sir that we – that I – am mystified. And concerned.'

'As am I,' said Will. He observed Montagu closely when he spoke again. 'For I suspect that my brother's life is in danger.'

James Montagu was suddenly alert, the louche attitude gone and he leant forward. 'How so? What have you heard?'

Will recounted to him his attack in the alleyway and how he was certain he had been mistaken for his brother.

'My dear man,' said Montagu. 'If you will allow me, I will take you to a man of medicine to tend that arm of yours and then we shall find you some other accommodation.' He glanced around the room. 'If your brother left here in such a hurry, then it may not be safe for you to stay here; you do closely resemble him, after all. And I'd wager you'd appreciate some fresh attire and a chance to rest and bathe.'

Will sighed. 'You are most kind, but I have already found alternative accommodation. Indeed, I was returning here to collect my belongings when I was set upon.'

James Montagu leapt to his feet. 'Then we shall visit the medical man forthwith and then after you have been treated, I shall take you back to your new lodgings.' He gestured towards the window. 'My carriage is outside.'

Will glanced out of the window and saw, on the opposite side of the street, a small two- seater phaeton carriage, with a street urchin holding the horse's head. He allowed himself a brief grin.

I doubt that Mr Montagu will want to drive through Seven Dials!

'Then I accept gratefully. But I have to own that I have little coin to pay a doctor.'

James Montagu looked momentarily discomfited but he recovered himself quickly. 'It will be my privilege to be of help, sir.'

Will took his leave of Mrs Baxter and Betsy and told them where he would be lodged for the next few days. Mrs Baxter said nothing but pursed her lips in disapproval.

'If my brother should come back here, Madame, would you be so good as to tell him where to find me.'

Mrs Baxter nodded – and sniffed.

Montagu said nothing but as soon as they were in the street, he turned to Will.

'Captain Fraser,' he said. 'You cannot lodge in Seven Dials. Why it is naught but a rookery. When we have seen the medical man, I will take you somewhere suitable.'

Will shook his head. He was feeling faint – and somewhat angry with the man's assumptions. Before they crossed the street to mount the phaeton, he stopped and turned to Montagu.

'I do not think you understand my situation, Sir. I am no longer a soldier; I have no rank and no pension.'

'But I thought …'

'You thought?'

Montagu frowned. 'I understood that you were a distinguished soldier, that you had served with honour in the Peninsular.'

'From whom did you glean this information?'

'Why, from your brother, of course. We often spoke of our families. He … he was mighty proud of you.'

For a moment, Will was overcome with fury at being brought to this situation and felt a deep sadness, too, that Jack's illusions must be shattered.

'My brother is probably not aware of recent events,' he said quietly.

James Montagu said no more. They crossed the street in silence and climbed into the phaeton; James tossed a coin to the urchin then took the reins. They turned West and then North and were soon in wider streets and in an altogether more affluent area of the city where they visited a doctor of Montagu's acquaintance who treated Will's wound using cotton batting soaked in carbolic acid and then expertly bound it, urging Will to ensure that the dressing was regularly changed. It did feel a deal more comfortable and Will thanked James.

'I will do all I can to help you, Fraser,' he said. 'But I would ask for your help, too.'

'My help? How can I help you? I am an impoverished man with no rank.'

James concentrated on guiding the horse past a crossing sweeper and some slow carts, then he turned to Will. 'I must find your brother,' he said quietly. 'Believe me, much depends on it.' He hesitated. 'He will find out that you are returned and my belief is that he will come looking for you. I beg you to tell me at once if he should contact you.'

'You say much depends on finding him. What do you mean by that?'

'I told you,' said Montagu. 'We both work for King George's Government, Jack and I. That is all you need to know.'

And with that, Will had to be content for, though he pressed James Montagu for further information, none was forthcoming. At length they made their way back to Seven Dials and Will's modest accommodation. James eyed the rude doorway with distaste and urged Will, once again, to find something more suited to his class, but Will would not be moved.

'It will suffice for now,' he said.

And I will be close to Armstrong.

As Will climbed out of the phaeton, James leant down and pressed a purse into his hand. 'Take it,' he whispered. 'If you find your brother, you will be furthering the work of the Government and believe me, there will be many who will be in your debt.'

'I cannot repay you.'

'I understand that.' He handed Will an embossed card. 'Be sure to contact me if you have news of him.'

And then he was gone, driving his horse through the muddle of hawkers, drunks, thieves and prostitutes that made up the population of Seven Dials, some ragged boys running after his phaeton, offering him their services, their goods, their mothers or sisters.

Will shoved the card and the purse of coin deep into his coat pocket, hoping that no one had witnessed the exchange, but instead of entering his lodgings, he turned down the street that led to The Haycart. He felt a strong urge to speak to someone he trusted about this strange turn of events.

Armstrong was not at the tavern so Will spent some time speaking with the motley collection of men there. At first they were suspicious of him but when one of the ex-soldiers let slip that he knew of Will's disgrace, they began to warm to him. A disgraced officer was no better than a thief or a drunk, after all. He was one of them. Nonetheless, Will was relieved when Armstrong appeared, scowling, with his head bent, until he saw Will and greeted him as he shrugged off his coat and sat down beside him.

'You look downcast, Sergeant,' said Will.

'I'm a man of action, sir. I can't sit on my bum all day quaffing beer, waiting for my pension, but it seems there's precious little work to be had round here – and none for a cripple like me.'

Will frowned. 'You're worth ten men, Sergeant, even with one arm.'

'You're the only man I know who'd say that.'

Will ordered them ale and then leant forward. 'I would talk to you in private, Sergeant. Is there some quiet place we can go?'

Armstrong raised his eyes to the ceiling. 'Quiet! You'd be lucky to find any quiet round here!' Then he narrowed his eyes. 'Have you some intelligence about your brother?'

'Not exactly,' said Will. 'But there has been a development.' He cast his eyes round the crowded room. 'It's getting dark and I'd rather not walk outside. Would the landlord let us use his back parlour for a time?'

Armstrong shrugged. 'That grubby little foxhole! I suppose he might but he'd expect payment.'

'I have coin,' said Will quietly.

Armstrong looked up sharply. 'But this morning you were down to your last penny. How…?

'Never mind.'

After some haggling, the landlord pleading that it was inconvenient and Will offering a little more coin, they secured the room for an hour and the man promised to leave them undisturbed.

'Well,' said Armstrong, sitting down on the hard chair in the dark little room and stretching his legs under the table. 'This is all very strange, sir.'

But when Will related all that had happened, Armstrong gave him his full attention.

'Bugger me, you could have been killed!'

Will nodded. 'Those villains clearly thought I was my brother and I fear he is in grave danger.'

'And do you trust this man Montagu?'

'Yes, I think he's true. He's as anxious to find Jack as I am.'

'And you say this Montagu fellow and your brother work for the Government?'

Will met Armstrong's eyes and there was a beat of silence.

'Yes,' said Will slowly.

'A Government man who disappears suddenly and who is being sought by his quality friend and some murdering thugs.'

'Yes,' said Will again.

'Are you thinking what I am thinking?'

'Possibly,' said Will, not taking his eyes from Armstrong's face. He took a deep breath and glanced toward the door, then leant nearer.

'If Jack is working for the Government,' he said very quietly, 'it is possible, I suppose, that he may have crossed those who are working against it.'

'Frenchies?'

'Possibly,' said Will. 'Though in truth I know nothing of the machinations of Government. It is merely the vaguest suspicion.'

'You think your brother is a spy? A spy for the Government?'

'As I say, it is only the vaguest notion.'

'But a solid notion. And if that is so, then with your resemblance to him ...'

Will nodded. 'Then I, too, may be in danger and that is one of many reasons why I must find him.' He frowned. 'And there's something else.'

'Yes?'

'A woman has been looking for him and she says she is his wife.'

'Your brother is married?'

Will shook his head. 'Not as far as I know.'

'This is a curious business, sir.'

'Curious indeed.'

Will dug the purse from his coat pocket and counted out the money on the table. Armstrong's eyes widened. 'Your brother's friend Montagu is mighty anxious for you to find him. That's a good haul of coin.'

Will, too, was surprised at how much the purse contained. 'If Montagu is paying me to search for Jack, then I must not disappoint.' He put the purse away. 'But I shall need help, Sergeant.'

Armstrong grinned. 'Indeed you will, sir.'

Chapter Four

They talked some more, making plans and rejecting them and had come to no conclusion as to a way forward when the landlord interrupted them saying that their hour was up and he needed the room. They re-joined the crush of men in the tavern and then went out to a pie and mash house for food.

Will felt stronger when he had eaten but both his head and his arm throbbed.

'You should get some sleep, sir,' said Armstrong. 'You're pale as a girl.'

Armstrong went with him as far as the door of Will's lodgings and they agreed to meet up in the morning.

'Take care,' said Will, glancing at the noisy crowds who seemed more threatening now darkness had fallen.

Armstrong looked around him and nodded at a foot patrol not far away. 'I reckon I'll be safe enough with those fellows about,' he said. Then he made a mock salute and hurried off.

Despite the snores and farts of the other men, the hard mattress and the thin blanket, exhaustion overcame Will and he slept well, his last waking thought of Jack and of his so called 'wife'.

Who the hell is this woman?

He awoke cold and stiff but, although his wounded arm felt bruised and sore, it no longer throbbed. Compared to this lodging, Mrs Baxter's house was the height of luxury. Here there were no victuals offered and when Will sought some way to wash, he found only a rusting pump in the filthy little yard outside the back door which produced just a dribble of evil smelling water.

When the Sergeant arrived, they were about to set off in search of some food when Will heard his name called.

'Mr Fraser, sir!'

Although it was a woman's voice, Will tensed and he whipped round. Then his shoulders relaxed as he spied one of the actresses from Mrs Baxter's lodging house.

'Sally! Whatever brings you to this rookery?'

Sally was out of breath. She raised her hand in greeting and then, ignoring the leers of some of the ruffians nearby, she came up to him. 'Believe me, sir, I'd not come here by choice but I thought you should know ...' Then she stopped and looked nervously towards Armstrong.

Will smiled. 'Sally, this is my good friend Sergeant Armstrong. Sergeant, this is Sally, who lodges where Jack used to stay. She's an actress,' he added.

Armstrong looked delighted and if he could have rubbed his hands together, he would have. 'An actress you say. Now that's a mighty hard profession for a pretty lass like you,' he began.

'Never mind that,' said Sally, curtly. She turned back to Will. 'I've come with some news,' she said.

Will was immediately alert. 'Of Jack?'

'No, but we had another visit from the woman last evening.'

'The woman who says she is his wife?'

Sally nodded. 'She was in such a state, frantic to find Mr Jack. Begged us to tell her anything we knew. Well Betsy had just opened her gob and I knew she was going to tell her all about you and say where you were lodged but I wasn't sure you'd want that.'

'Thank you, Sally. You were right not to reveal my whereabouts. After what happened yesterday, I trust no one.'

Sally nodded. 'Umm, I thought so. Anyways, I dug Betsy in the ribs and scowled at her and I said to the lady that I might have something to tell her if she came back to Ma Baxter's this afternoon. She looked ever so grateful and said she'd return then.'

'And you took the trouble to come over to this den of thieves to warn me? Truly Sally, I am in your debt.' Will frowned. 'I trust you were not followed here – or molested in any way?'

'Nothing I couldn't deal with,' said Sally. 'Though, to be truthful this place makes me nervous. I asked Lottie to come with me but she was going after some job she'd heard about.'

'Then the least we can do is to give you some refreshment.'

Sally looked at him. 'You said you were down to your last penny.'

Will smiled. 'Ah, well, I had some good fortune.'

'And would this good fortune have anything to do with that fancy gent who came to see you yesterday? Betsy told us all about him.'

'You are the most observant of young women,' said Will.

After the three of them had found a place to serve them some bread and tea, the men offered to escort Sally back to Drury Lane.

'I had thought to go to Covent Garden,' she said. 'To have a look at what's happening at the Royal. There's always some theatricals hanging round there and they may have news of work to be had.'

'Then the Captain and I will escort you,' said Armstrong. 'I'll wager we'll just be cooling our heels until we meet up with this mystery woman.'

'Will you stop calling me Captain,' hissed Will. 'And I'll thank you not to take decisions on my behalf.'

Armstrong raised an eyebrow but said nothing.

As they strolled away from Seven Dials the crowds lessened and they were able to have a conversation without being jostled this way and that.

'What do you know of James Montagu, Sally?' asked Will.

'The fancy gent with the phaeton?' She shrugged. 'Nothing of note. Since Mr Jack left, Betsy says he's been to the house a few times.'

'And did he visit my brother before then?'

She frowned. 'I can't say. Mr Jack had visitors but in truth me and Lottie were out most evenings so I can't say if Mr Montagu was one of them.'

'And this mystery woman?'

'Well, I never saw her before Mr Jack went but that's not to say she didn't visit him.'

At length they reached Covent Garden. There were stalls everywhere of all sorts of produce, and hawkers calling out their wares and there, behind all the activity, stood the burnt- out shell of the Theatre Royal. They stood and looked at it for a while, watching workmen heaving out blackened seating and ornaments and richly coloured curtains. Sally sighed.

'I got good memories of that place,' she said. 'We had some fine times there – and we got paid regular, not like in some of the dumps where me and Lottie have worked.' Then suddenly she caught sight of a gaggle of folk on the other side of the square, talking and gesticulating. 'Hey, I know them,' she said, and picking up her skirts she ran over and had soon joined in the animated conversation.

Armstrong watched her go. 'She's a fine lass, that one.'

'Don't you go getting ideas Sergeant, we have work to do.'

But Armstrong continued to watch her as she partook in lively conversation with her friends. At length she came over to them.

'There's talk of work at the theatre in Drury Lane,' she said. 'We enquired a few weeks ago, just after the fire, but now there's a rumour they're putting on a new show and they'll be hiring again.'

'That would suit well, would it not,' said Will. 'Being so close to Mrs Baxter's lodging house.'

She nodded. 'Wish me luck,' she said. 'We're going over there now.'

'Don't forget your assignation with our mystery woman,' said Will.

'I'll be at the house to greet her at three o'clock sharp.'

'And remember. I want to have sight of her before revealing myself,' said Will.

Sally tapped her head. 'I won't forget.'

'And our signal?'

'I'll remember.'

For the rest of the morning and during the early afternoon, Will and Armstrong wandered about, acquainting themselves with the area around Drury Lane and seeking out a position where they could observe, unseen, the woman who called herself Jack's wife, as she approached Mrs Baxter's house. And, at Armstrong's urging, Will purchased them both a short dagger.

'I couldn't handle a sword with only one arm but you are more handy with a sword, sir,' said Armstrong. 'Are you sure …'

Will shook his head. 'I have been observing the crowds,' he said. 'No men have swords at their sides now. I would stand out horribly.'

A full fifteen minutes before three, they were huddled in a narrow gap between the houses opposite Mrs Baxter's. It afforded them a good view of the street in both directions and Will, mindful of his recent experience, had insisted that they walk up and down its length to assure themselves that there were no villains lurking there. As they waited, Will let his thoughts wander to the childhood in the North which he and Jack had shared. Jack always the quiet one, the scholar, the thoughtful one while Will had been the boy who relished adventure, always getting himself into scrapes. Then his thoughts were interrupted as Armstrong dug him in the ribs.

'There's a woman coming,' he said. 'And she's in a great hurry.'

But as she drew near the house, he let out his breath. 'Ah, it's just young Sally.'

Will smiled. 'I knew she wouldn't let us down.'

'Aye, she's a rare good girl.'

'Keep your eyes skinned, Sergeant. I'll look up the street, you look down.'

In the distance, they could hear the chimes of one of the nearby churches striking three o'clock and although there were folk walking up and down the street, no one stopped at Mrs Baxter's door. The minutes ticked by and Will began to feel uneasy.

What if this is some elaborate trick? What if this woman is associated with the villains who attacked me?

But just then he noticed a woman approaching and, even from a distance, her walk and the way in which she carried herself seemed familiar to him. As she came closer, he could see that she was wearing a dark bonnet secured with a bow under her chin and that a veil was covering her face. But he knew her immediately.

He drew in his breath sharply and his heart started to beat faster. He clenched his fists.

Surely it cannot be?

She stopped at Mrs Baxter's door but even as she raised her hand to knock, Sally slipped out to speak to her.

Will lunged forward, about to race across the street towards her but Armstrong put a hand on his arm to stop him 'Do you recognise her, sir?'

'Yes,' said Will shortly. 'Yes, I know her well.'

Armstrong gave a whistle; Sally heard it and looked over. She exchanged a few quick words with the woman and then, taking her arm, she led her across to the men.

As she approached, Will was transported back to a time when he was a callow youth with ambitions above his station and a hopeless love for Clara, the daughter of the landowner from whom his father rented their farm. The blood rushed to his cheeks as he remembered the time when he had summoned the courage to express his love for her and lay bare his feelings.

Feelings she had not returned.

How can I still be so affected?

And then, as Sally ran back to the house, Clara was there in front of him, putting up her veil, coming forward to embrace him but, of a sudden, gasping and stepping back, tears springing to her eyes. At last Will found his voice. 'Clara!'

'Will,' she said, her voice choked. 'Your resemblance to Jack is more striking than ever. Why, for a moment I almost believed …'

She is nervous. And she looks pale and unwell.

Will swallowed. 'Is it true? Are you and Jack married?'

She did not answer directly but looked at Armstrong. 'Who is your companion?'

'Sergeant Armstrong. We were together in the Peninsular and he is utterly to be trusted. Sergeant, this is Miss Clara Wylie.'

She turned back to Will then and met his eyes.

'No, no longer Miss Wylie. I am Mrs Jack Fraser now.'

Will looked away, trying to recover himself, then at last he spoke again. 'When? When did you marry? What has happened to Jack?'

She looked up and down the street. 'Can we not go inside Mrs Baxter's house,' she said.

Will shook his head. 'I am not welcome there and I believe that I am in some danger in this area. Then as they stood huddled together in the dark alleyway strewn with rubbish, he told her of what had happened since he had come to London.

Clara put a hand on his arm. 'I am so sorry, Will, but this is not your concern and I warrant you will soon be gone back to your regiment and removed from this turmoil.'

'I am no longer a soldier, Clara.'

She looked shocked. 'What? How can that be. It is all you lived for!'

Armstrong interrupted. 'He was betrayed, Madame, and sorely used.'

Will put up a hand. 'It is a long story, Clara, and our pressing need is to find Jack. Do you have any intelligence of where he might be? And when did you marry? I would have thought he would have sent me word.'

Clara shivered and held her cloak more closely round her shoulders. 'He did send word, Will, but obviously it did not reach you.' She went on. 'Jack and I had had an understanding for some time but it was our secret. He wanted to establish himself so that he might earn my father's consent to our union. So he came to London a year ago and was lucky to be recommended to a post in the Government.' She smiled. 'You know he has a fine mind and, like you, he has a facility with languages.'

Will nodded. 'Jack was always the better scholar,' he said.

Clara continued. 'In short, he established himself and was being well paid and when he came North to ask for my hand, my father consented.'

'When was this?'

'We had a quiet wedding just over a month ago. Jack has a lawyer friend who found us an apartment in New Square in Lincoln's Inn, which is where I am living.'

'Then why?'

'Why did he continue to keep his room at Mrs Baxter's?' Clara sighed. 'In truth, it seemed an extravagance, but he said he could see people there who he'd rather I did not meet. Who he did not want coming to our door.'

Will frowned and Clara went on. 'As you can imagine, I was not happy with this arrangement for often he'd be away for the night, and when I pressed him he said that there were things he could not tell me, things that involved the security of the country.'

Armstrong looked up sharply. 'Then he *is* a spy!'

'*Sergeant*,' whispered Will.

Clara nodded. 'I had begun to come to that conclusion myself and realised I could not press him for answers.' She cleared her throat and continued. 'Sally told me just now that you have met up with Montagu?' When Will nodded, Clara went on. 'Montagu came sometimes to Lincoln's Inn and he and Jack would always be in close discussion, but now even Montagu knows nothing of his whereabouts.'

'Nor you, evidently,' said Will.

Clara bit her lip and it cut Will to the quick to see her eyes fill with tears again. 'And yet he swore to me, on his life, that he would never leave me in ignorance. That wherever he was, he would somehow send word that he was safe.'

'And you have heard nothing.'

She shook her head. 'Nothing for over a week.'

Will frowned and stroked his chin. 'What puzzles me, Clara, is why Montagu thinks I can find Jack and why he gave me such a generous supply of coin to do so.'

Clara shivered again. 'By the nature of his employment, I would guess that James Montagu has informants everywhere,' she said. 'He would have been told of your arrival and of your resemblance to Jack.'

'But if he and his informants have no intelligence of Jack's whereabouts, why should he think that I would do any better? He will have to give me some inkling of Jack's work and what his mission was.'

All three of them were silent for a moment, then Armstrong spoke up.

'Want to know what I think?'

'What's that Sergeant?'

Armstrong scratched the stump of his arm. 'I think this fancy friend of yours wants you to be a decoy.'

'What!' Both Clara and Will looked at him in astonishment.

Chapter Five

'Think on it,' said Armstrong. 'A Jack Fraser in two different places. A puzzle for any of England's enemies.'

Will couldn't help but smile. 'That is beyond fanciful Sergeant!'

But Clara looked thoughtful. 'Have you arranged to meet Montagu again, Will?'

'We have no formal arrangement, but I have his card and he asked me to report any news to him. And he knows where I lodge.'

'He'll be finding out about you Will, mark my words,' said Clara. 'And then he'll reel you in like a fish. He may present as a dandy about town with his modish clothes and his drawling voice, but he's a clever, devious fellow. He'll want his money's worth and if you don't go to him then he'll seek you out again soon enough.'

Clara was shivering but Will could not tell whether it was from cold or fear.

'You should go home, Clara,' he said. 'The Sergeant and I shall escort you.'

She shook her head. 'My carriage is in the next street. I asked the driver to wait out of sight of Mrs Baxter's house just in case…'

'In case?'

'I am afraid, Will. And so should you be!'

Will smiled. 'I've faced death many times,' he said.

'And from what you say, you've just dodged it again, but on English soil,' said Clara quietly. She took his hand for a moment. 'Be careful, dear Will. You know where I am but unless you have any definite intelligence, I think it would be wise to avoid coming to our home.'

Will put her hand to his lips and she let it rest there for a moment before pulling it gently away then walking off briskly down the street and round the corner.

Will watched her until she was out of sight.

Armstrong cleared his throat. 'A shock was it, sir, to hear she's married to your brother?'

Slowly, Will turned and focussed on the Sergeant. He frowned and nodded. 'I … I can scarce believe it,' he said quietly. 'I had no idea they had an understanding.'

'Changes things, does it sir?'

Will braced his shoulders. 'No, of course not. Meeting with Clara has simply reinforced my determination to find Jack. If he has left her in ignorance of his whereabouts, then …'

'Then?'

'Then something is clearly awry. But I am at a loss as to how to proceed.

'The lady said that the man Montagu would seek you out, did she not?'

Will leant back against the wall of the alley. 'Aye, but I am minded to forestall him, Sergeant. I need to know more from him and I need to understand why Jack is a target for attack. I feel that I am stumbling in a fog of misinformation with one hand tied behind my back.'

'Then you know how I feel,' said Armstrong, grinning. And he was relieved to see Will's shoulders drop and his face relax into a slight smile.

'Shall we pay a visit to this fancy fellow, then, sir? I confess I am all agog.'

'Indeed we shall, Sergeant, and I would rather not delay it further.'

Will dug in the pocket of his coat and looked at the card Montagu had given him.

'His house is in Knightsbridge,' he said.

'How far is that?'

Will shrugged. 'I imagine it is not far from the place he took me to see that man of medicine. In any case, time is short. We shall hire a hackney cab.'

Armstrong raised his eyebrows but said nothing.

'If Montagu wants action, then he'll have to pay for it,' said Will grimly.

When the hackney cab drew up at the address Will had been given, the two men hesitated briefly before they approached the door. The paintwork was immaculate, the doorstep freshly scrubbed and the house overlooked a pleasant garden set in the middle of a square with some of the trees still in leaf where children played, accompanied by their nursemaids.

'He does well for himself, your friend,' muttered Armstrong.

Will did not reply but raised the brightly polished brass knocker and banged on the door.

When a maid answered the door and Will asked for Montagu, she went as if to close it saying her master had left instructions that he was not to be disturbed, but Will pushed past her into the hallway.

She looked nervous but he smiled at her. 'Please tell him that Will Fraser is here to see him.' Then, when she looked doubtful. 'He is awaiting my visit.'

The maid went quickly out of the room, glancing behind her once before she closed the door.

They did not have to wait long. Montagu came into the hall almost immediately and, for a man of such natural poise and elegance, he seemed a little flustered.

He shook Will's hand. 'A delightful surprise my dear sir,' he said. Then he turned to Armstrong. 'And your companion? I do not think I have made his acquaintance.'

'This is Sergeant Armstrong,' said Will.

There was a moment's awkward silence.

'He was with me in the Peninsular,' said Will.

'Ah.'

'And he is utterly to be trusted.'

Montagu glanced at Armstrong. 'Perhaps, Sergeant Armstrong, you would like to take some refreshment in the kitchen. I'm sure my cook will …'

'The Sergeant is going to help me in my endeavours to find my brother,' said Will firmly. 'Anything you tell me, I shall convey to him. I wish him to hear our conversation.'

Montagu gave the slightest shrug at this obvious breach of etiquette, but he did not argue and led them both into a pleasant morning room with deep bay windows looking out onto the square.

As Will sat down, he caught the whiff of something in the air. A familiar scent but one he could not recall smelling before in England. He frowned.

Montagu delayed things by insisting on calling for refreshments and watched Will closely as he raised a glass of fortified wine to his lips.

Montagu smiled. 'Not smuggled, I assure you,' he said. 'This was put down in the cellar long before the start of the war.'

'It is excellent,' said Will. He took another sip and looked around the room which was furnished, as was fashionable, in the French manner and he noted examples of old Sevres porcelain, inlaid tables, ormolu vases and other examples of French elegance.

'A charming room,' said Will.

Armstrong looked uncomfortable, perched on a dainty chair, and said nothing.

'Yes,' said Montagu, 'despite years of warfare and blockade, dealers still cross the Channel in search of bargains. There seems no end to the appetite in London for French decorative arts.'

Will thought fleetingly of his childhood home, the large and functional farmhouse in the North where such fripperies would have looked ridiculous and out of place.

Montagu rose from his seat and went to stand by the marble fireplace, warming his back at the blazing fire.

'Now my friend,' he said, looking at Will. 'I do have some urgent business to attend to today, so can I ask if you have made any progress in the search for Jack? Is that why you are here?'

'I have met with his wife,' said Will. 'But I have hardly had time to …'

'Ah yes, the lovely Clara. She is as bewildered as the rest of us.' Montagu cleared his throat. 'And that is all you have achieved? You have no ideas about a safe place to which he might have fled, friends he might have contacted?'

As he was seated, Will felt at a disadvantage while Montagu peered down at him so he, too, stood up.

'I feel I cannot proceed in my search for him, sir, without knowing something of his business. You say you both work for the Government but in what capacity? Why should his life be in danger? From whom? I will, I swear, do my best to track him down but you have already remarked on our close resemblance to one another. I need to know of his enemies and be alert to the possibility that they may mistake me for Jack and come after me again.'

There was a long silence while Montagu stared out of the window. Somewhere in the house a clock chimed the hour.

'And why me?' continued Will. 'I am nothing now but a disgraced ex-soldier. Surely there are others – Government people perhaps – who could search for him with more authority?'

'Ah,' said Montagu at last. 'Then I see that I shall have to speak more freely, but first I must ask you to swear that no hint of what I am about to reveal to you will ever leave this room.'

Will swallowed. 'I know how to keep a secret,' he said. 'As does Sergeant Armstrong.'

Montagu's eyes rested on Armstrong for a moment, then he turned back to Will.

'Both of you must swear to me.'

'I give you my word,' said Will.

'Aye,' muttered Armstrong. 'And I. I can keep quiet when necessary.' His eyes caught Will's briefly and they both remembered another occasion when secrecy was paramount.

Montagu began to pace up and down then stopped again by the fireplace.

'Doubtless you are aware of the smuggling which takes place on the South coast?'

Will looked puzzled by the question and shrugged. 'I have certainly heard rumours,' he said.

'And what do these rumours say?'

'Well.' Will hesitated. 'I suppose it is only to be expected that since we are at war with France and with all the embargoes and blockades in place, there will be many opportunities for smugglers to ply their trade in contraband goods.'

Montagu nodded. 'Smuggling is rife,' he said. 'But they traffic more than contraband.'

'Are you saying that they …' began Will.

Montagu gave a humourless laugh. 'Contraband goods are the least of it,' he said. 'There is a thriving trade in much more dangerous cargoes.'

'Dangerous to this country?' asked Will, beginning to understand where the conversation was heading.

'You catch my drift exactly, Fraser. 'English smugglers not only subvert national borders and maritime blockades but if the price is right they have no qualms about betraying their country. They are trafficking spies, information and escaping French prisoners of war across the Channel. And even, on occasion, supplying Napoleon's troops with firearms. They have no loyalty and no conscience and will work for whoever pays them good coin.'

'That is shocking, sir.'

Montagu suddenly thumped his fist down on a nearby table, startling the other two men.

'More than shocking! It is undermining the Government's whole network of undercover work and information gathering. The Customs officers do their best but even some of them are susceptible to bribery. And now they say that Napoleon is going to establish an English smuggling base at Gravelines.'

'I had no idea,' began Will.

'But that is not the worst of it, Fraser.'

'No?'

'No. This smuggling of spies has been going on since the wars began. We have our own spies in France and we disseminate false information to throw the French off the scent, as they do to us. And I pride myself that we are better at it than our enemies and more subtle in our subterfuges. It is largely a game of cat and mouse. We catch and punish smuggling gangs but they are well organised and have many secret places where they stash their goods and from where they set off with the human cargoes across the Channel. Even so, they are often caught and we successfully extract information from them.'

Will looked at Armstrong. Both men could imagine the process of such extraction.

'No,' continued Montagu. 'It is a recent turn of events that is far more worrying.'

Will said nothing but continued to watch Montagu, and Clara's words came back to him: *'He may present as a dandy about town with his modish clothes and his drawling voice, but he's a clever, devious fellow.'*

'Just before you arrived back on these shores, Fraser, we discovered that a carefully planned and extensive plot to undermine Napoleon's leadership, seems to have been unmasked. I cannot reveal the details to you but suffice it to say that it had been months in the planning and that only those at the highest level knew of it – both in the British Government and within our network and the Royalist conspirators in France with whom we collaborate. All the details were in place and only the most trusted of our agents knew of it. These agents have never let us down and so we have had to conclude that the traitor is … elsewhere.'

'Elsewhere?'

For the first time since they had met, Will saw another side to Montagu. Gone was the fashionable, louche dandy. Now there was passion in his speech and fury in his eyes. 'I cannot believe that any of those agents who we trusted with this secret plan have revealed it.'

Armstrong spoke up then. 'So, sir, you are saying that there may be a traitor within the British Government?'

'Yes, Sergeant, I think that is a possibility. And it will be someone close to power for only those at the highest level knew of the plan.'

Will frowned. 'And what was Jack's part in all this?'

'Your brother and I work closely with our agents.'

'Then he *is* a spy,' said Armstrong.

'He and I run the network. As you can imagine, his fluency in the French language is very useful and he is an excellent judge of what is true or false in the documents we capture.'

'What do you think has happened to him?'

Montagu sighed. 'He disappeared so suddenly that I can only imagine that our traitor discovered that Jack suspected him and will make every effort to silence him.'

Will rubbed his arm, still sore from the recent attack. He had every reason to believe that this was the case.

'And Jack told you nothing of his suspicions?'

Montagu shrugged. 'I confess that I am surprised that he has sent no word to me but his disappearance was so sudden and it may be that he feared that any communication would be intercepted. And no doubt he would be right if the man he suspects is so powerful and has influence in Government. My belief is that Jack has gone to ground while trying to gather proof of his suspicions.'

'Or he is already dead,' said Armstrong.

Montagu nodded. 'Again, that is a possibility,' he said slowly.

There was a heavy silence in the room, only broken by the buzzing of a fly banging itself against a windowpane.

It was Armstrong who spoke first. 'But why Captain Fraser? Why should you ask him to find his brother?'

Montagu examined his hands then said. 'Since meeting you Fraser, I have made it my business to find out more about you.' He paused. 'I know what happened to you in Portugal.'

Will frowned. 'My disgrace is not connected to my brother,' he said quietly.

'No, indeed. But from what I have heard you acted honourably and were betrayed and put into an impossible situation.'

'That jealous bastard,' Armstrong muttered.

'It is all in the past, Sergeant,' said Will.

'Indeed,' said Montagu, 'but it may be that I can have some influence …' He didn't finish the sentence and continued to examine his hands.

'Are you saying you could get him pardoned sir?' asked Armstrong, the delicate chair creaking as he swivelled round to face Montagu.

'No, no, I would make no promises to that effect, obviously. I am merely saying that I could perhaps have a word in an influential ear and ask that the circumstances be more thoroughly investigated …'

Armstrong's face was red. 'So it's a bribe, then. Find your brother for me and I'll get your case looked at.'

'Hush Sergeant,' said Will. 'I think you are forgetting something.'

'Eh? What's that then?'

'That I love my brother and I want to find him.'

Montagu smiled. 'And that, Fraser, is why I am asking you to help us.'

'Us?'

'The British Government.'

Chapter Six

It was early evening by the time Will and Armstrong left the Knightsbridge house. Montagu's urgent appointment had been forgotten and the three men had set about constructing a plan. Will had racked his brains to think of places where Jack might be hiding but he could only think of those in the North, empty barns, deserted cottages and the like which he and Jack had explored as youngsters. Montagu, however, had insisted that, if Jack was still alive, he would have travelled South, almost certainly to the coast, where he would have the best chance of following a lead and finding informers among the smuggling gangs.

Montagu reiterated that because of Will's close relationship with Jack, if he found his brother then Jack would trust him.

'He will trust no one now, least of all those close to power. But you, Fraser, he will trust and if he has aught to tell me, he will know you can be relied upon to relay it to me.'

Montagu then gave Will the details of a code he could use when doing this. He explained that it was a new code which had not been used before and to which only Montagu was privy.

'In these circumstances, Fraser, I can trust no-one else for I have no idea who has betrayed us and it is of the utmost urgency that we root out the traitor before he does more harm. And to do that we must find your brother.' Montagu frowned. 'I fear that Jack has decided he can act alone to find proof of this man's treachery and bring him to justice, but he must not. Jack is a scholar and a diplomat; he would not be able to defend himself if he were attacked. He would put himself in mortal harm.'

'Yes, I understand that.'

Just before they left, Montagu had looked closely at Will 'I wonder if you might consider.' Then he shook his head. 'No, it is too much to ask. I cannot expect it of you.'

'I can only refuse,' said Will.

'No … no it would be …'

'Oh, for God's sake, spit it out, man,' said Armstrong, whose tongue had been considerably loosened by more of Montagu's excellent port.

'Well, Fraser, the more I look at you, the more I see the resemblance to your brother and …'

'What did I tell you, sir,' muttered Armstrong. 'He wants you to be a decoy!'

Montagu held up his hands. 'Not exactly,' he said. 'But … well you are a soldier and I hear a fine swordsman …'

'The best in the regiment,' said Armstrong, his words slightly slurred.

Will understood the implication. 'I can certainly defend myself,' he said slowly, 'if I were to be attacked. As can the Sergeant,' he continued, seeing Montagu glance at Armstrong's empty sleeve.

'Ah,' sighed Montagu. 'Then you perceive what I am suggesting, do you not? Your brother's hair is lighter and he is clean shaven but you are of the same build and with a little adjustment, you could easily pass for him.'

'So if the Captain is mistaken for his brother and set upon, he'd let you know, eh?' Armstrong folded his arms. 'That seems a queer sort of bargain.'

'I agree,' said Montagu. 'And it is only a suggestion which you are under no obligation to put into practice but if you could identify any such attackers, then that might give us some indication as to who has hired them.'

'I'll think on it,' said Will as they said their farewells. Montagu's servant had found them a hackney cab and as the driver urged his horse forward, Montagu stood at his door, his hand raised. 'Bonne chance, mes braves,' he whispered to himself. Then he turned and went inside.

For a while, as the hackney bowled along the wider streets of Knightsbridge and then slowed as the streets became more congested and the driver negotiated a way through carts and wagons, Will and Armstrong discussed, in low tones, all that they had been told.

'Will you do as he asks and adjust your appearance sir?'

'I wouldn't know how.'

Armstrong grinned. 'I fancy there's someone who could help you with that.'

'What do you mean?'

'Your little actress friend, sir. No doubt theatre folk know all about disguise and changing appearance.'

Will frowned. 'You may be right, Sergeant, but we are sworn to secrecy. If it gets abroad that I have changed my appearance …'

'Would you not trust young Sally, sir? I'd swear that she'd not squeal.'

'I don't know, Sergeant.'

'We could seek her out and ask if she'd do us a favour. I warrant she'd be mighty intrigued.'

Will raised an eyebrow. 'Hmm. Are your motives quite pure in this my friend? Is it not that you are looking for an excuse to be further acquainted with her?'

'I am only thinking of your interests, sir,' said Armstrong in a tone of offended innocence.

'Well, I suppose it could do no harm to approach her but she must know nothing of our plans.'

'Of course not. And you should not be seen near that house in Drury Lane. I'll call there myself.'

'Well …'

'Time is short, sir. We need to act quickly if it's to be done.'

Will needed some persuasion but eventually he agreed that Armstrong should be dropped off at the end of Drury Lane and go looking for Sally, and he himself would continue on to Seven Dials.

As they were approaching Drury Lane, Will remembered something.

'Sergeant, did you notice that smell when we entered Montagu's morning room?'

'Aye. Someone had been smoking a cigar.'

Will nodded. 'From what I understand, the habit has lately come to these shores from Portugal but it is not widespread. And cigars are expensive.'

'No doubt there's smuggling involved?'

'Perhaps,' said Will. 'But Montagu was not smoking himself and there was no sign of a half-smoked cigar in the room.'

'Then perhaps the smoker had been ushered out with undue haste.'

'Yes, that was my feeling. And Montagu did seem a trifle ruffled at our sudden appearance. It may be that he did not want us to see his visitor.'

In Drury Lane Armstrong descended from the cab and Will pressed some coin into his

hand before continuing on to Seven Dials. Darkness was falling and the driver was uneasy entering the rookery. He remarked to Will as he took payment, that it was no place for a gentleman.

'I agree my friend,' said Will. 'But then I am no gentleman.'

The driver shook his head and turned the cab away from Seven Dials with obvious relief as Will entered the Haycart tavern and settled down to wait for Armstrong's return. As he did so he pondered all that he had learnt from James Montagu.

It was a strange assignment and no doubt fraught with danger if he was to be the decoy to draw the Government's enemies from their cover. But then, what choice did he have? He wanted to find Jack and, if what Montagu said was true, if he succeeded then some important people would be in his debt, which could possibly be to his advantage. Montagu had insisted that Jack was most likely to have travelled down to the coast to make enquiries among the smuggling gangs and Will had been given money and had been promised more, together with a sword and firearm, for his journey South.

He'd always been drawn to adventure and he'd have a loyal friend by his side.

And yet. There was something about this quest which did not sit easy with him and for the life of him he could not fathom what it was; a whiff of something not quite right, like the lingering smell of that cigar smoke.

He looked about him, greeting some of the familiar faces in the tavern. Although he knew he'd never be considered one of them, they had, to a certain extent, accepted him and he'd even struck up a sort of friendship with one or two of the ruffians who jostled and drank and spat and laughed beside him.

He spent the time profitably, talking to a trio of men who seemed to have some knowledge of the smuggling fraternity on the South coast and he hinted to them that he might have access to a commodity which could be taken across the Channel. To his amusement, none of them seemed in any way surprised at this. He was a disgraced and penniless ex officer and it was natural to them that his next step would be to turn to crime. He listened and absorbed their stories, peppered with outrageous descriptions of the smuggling families and the subterfuges they'd developed for avoiding the law. He bought his companions ale and they remarked how he appeared to have come by more coin, but they didn't pry further, just rubbed the side of their noses in understanding and eagerly accepted his largesse.

Over an hour had passed when, at last, Armstrong reappeared, breathless and flushed. He greeted the boisterous crowd and then took Will to one side and whispered in his ear.

'No time to waste, sir. The girls are outside.'

'The girls?'

'Sally and Lottie. We're in luck. Sal got hold of some dye and whatnot from the ruins of the Royal this afternoon. It was being thrown out and she took it in case she got work and needed it.'

'They are both here?'

Armstrong nodded. 'I told them what was needed and they're all agog.'

Now two more souls know I am to become my brother.

Quick sir, I don't like to leave them outside but – and here he looked round at the rough men singing and swearing and making merry – it's better than in here.'

Thinking of the girls' predicament, Will had little choice but to follow Armstrong outside. 'We'll leave at first light,' he said. 'I don't want to be seen again in this place with a changed appearance.'

'I'd thought of that,' said Armstrong. 'I called in at your lodgings and bribed those two fellows you share with to get out for the night. We can go there.'

Will laughed. 'You are astonishingly resourceful, Sergeant!'

When they got outside the tavern, Sally and Lottie were in heated conversation with some
drunks and looked up with relief to see Will and Armstrong. At their appearance, the two drunks staggered away, muttering obscenities.

'Fools!' said Sally. Then she continued, addressing Will. 'I don't know why you choose to lodge here sir, it's no place for a gentleman.'

'So I keep being told.'

'I brought Lottie along 'cos she's more skilled at the painting and dyeing.'

They reached Will's lodgings and found no one about except the landlady who was already well in her cups. She leered at the party.

'It's not what you think,' hissed Lottie, her eyes flashing. 'We're decent girls.'

The woman smirked and took another swig of her drink.

'I'm sorry,' whispered Will, as he ushered the girls into his room. 'We have put you in a difficult position and I would not for the world …'

'Oh hush,' said Sally. 'We want to help you find Mr Jack, don't we Lottie?'

Lottie nodded and looked about her. 'This is a right hovel,' she said. 'And I'll need more light.'

The ever-resourceful Armstrong was sent to obtain more candles from the landlady and returned not only with a further supply but also with a lantern. Lottie and Sally set to work, chatting and giggling together as they discussed Jack's appearance.

'He wears his hair shorter than you and it's a fair bit lighter,' said Lottie, busying herself with scissors and stopping to admire her handiwork from time to time. 'And I've never seen him with a beard.'

'That's easily put right,' said Will. 'I have shaving equipment in my haversack.'

Lottie produced a small phial of liquid.

'What is this?' asked Will.

'Peroxide,' she said. 'It's new in the theatre but it's a strong bleach. I've seen how it takes the colour out.'

She mixed the contents into a bowl of water and made Will dunk his head in it and leave it there a while. Later, she attacked his bushy eyebrows with tweezers to make them smoother and better defined.

'Shall you need to dye them too,' asked Will, nervous that the acid would dribble down into his eyes.

She shook her head. 'I remember Jack as having quite dark eyebrows.'

It took a long while but at last the girls were satisfied. They made Will turn this way and that and held the lantern up to examine him. Finally, they found a mirror and Will looked at himself.

'You've transformed me,' he said, laughing. 'It is as if Jack is staring back at me.'

'There's just one more thing,' said Lottie, producing a jar of cream.

'What's this?'

'Your complexion is a little darker. If you rub this into your face each night, it should lighten your skin.'

Will stared suspiciously at the jar. 'And what does this contain?'

Lottie shrugged. 'I don't rightly know. But I've seen it used to good effect.'

Gingerly, Will took it though he doubted he'd use it.

It was well after midnight when Will and Armstrong escorted the girls back to Drury Lane and impressed upon them the need for secrecy.

'Don't worry, sir. We can keep our mouths shut.'

'Will Mrs Baxter turn you out soon?' asked Will, as Sally and Lottie let themselves into the house.

Lottie shrugged. 'We're after a couple of jobs and she's said she'll let us stay until we hear whether we've got them.'

Will was anxious to leave the vicinity of Mrs Baxter's house and he glanced fearfully down dark alleyways as they headed back but there was no-one about to molest them. Once they reached Seven Dials, Armstrong left Will at the door of his lodgings.

'Well Captain, he said, grinning into the darkness, 'Our adventure begins!'

Chapter Seven

Later that evening, in another part of London, another meeting took place.

There was no need for the two men concerned to meet in secret. They were both in the same line of work, albeit one more junior than the other, and their paths crossed frequently. This meeting, however, was different. Everything had changed between them and the atmosphere of menace in the room was palpable.

The older man, shrewd, impressive and utterly ruthless, was in a rage, though to observe his outward appearance, a casual onlooker would not have known it. He stood tall, his hands clasped behind his back, and stared impassively at his companion.

'I shall ask you again,' he said. 'How, in God's name, could you have allowed this to happen?'

His companion tried not to flinch. Although more frightened than he had ever been in his life, he held his ground.

'I hardly think it fair to accuse me of allowing it to happen, sir. After all, it was you who sent the letter.

The older man narrowed his eyes. 'As you very well know,' he said, his voice unnervingly quiet, 'I was out of London at the time. It was the only way I could communicate with you.'

The younger man's voice was full of bitterness. 'I still contend that it was not necessary to send a letter. You had already conveyed your wishes to me verbally and you had left me in little doubt that, if I valued my life, I had no choice but to betray my country.'

The older man waved his hand in dismissal of this logical reply, and continued.

'I needed to make sure you understood your obligations clearly.' He hesitated. 'But you already had your suspicions about Fraser, did you not.' It was a statement, not a question.

'No, I had no idea …'

'Liar!' The word was uttered explosively and a tiny globule of spittle followed it and settled on the cuff of the younger man's sleeve.

He did not reply immediately but busied himself in wiping at the spittle with a handkerchief. It irritated him that he could not stop the trembling in his hand.

'No sir, I am no liar,' he replied at length. 'And nor am I convinced that Fraser has any knowledge of your identity.'

'Of *course* he does, you fool! Why else has he vanished together with that letter? There is not a fraction of doubt that he took it. He knows that if I were to be unmasked then it would put an end to all my work, and what an achievement that would be for him, eh? And that letter is all the proof he needs. Indeed, it is the *only* proof.'

His companion cleared his throat. 'We do not *know* that it was he who intercepted it, sir. And even if he did, he would not be able to decipher it. He has no knowledge of the new chemicals needed to bring the secret writing to light.'

For a moment the older man looked thoughtful.

'Yes, it is entirely possible, I suppose, that he has not yet deciphered it, but he is a clever man. It is only a matter of time before he does – or finds someone who already knows how to do so.'

'No one on this side of the Channel knows the ingredients necessary to unlock its secret.'

'Except you and I.'

'Except you and I.'

'Then, my friend, you must find Fraser forthwith - before he has a chance to read its contents.'

The younger man nodded, his face ashen. Then he looked up.

'Would you truly carry out your threat to reveal ...?'

There was a short silence before the other replied, his voice very quiet as he came close to the younger man and leant over him. 'You cannot deny that you are guilty.' Then when the other shook his head, he continued. 'If you do not kill Fraser and destroy that letter, then I swear to you that I shall have no compunction in revealing to the world your filthy secret, for if I am unmasked, then I will make it my business to unmask you, too.' Then he patted the other's cheek and the younger man flinched and drew away. 'And,' he continued, 'you would not survive such a revelation, would you? Which is why I know that you will do my bidding.'

Then, suddenly, he pushed his companion to one side and, without a backward glance, strode over to the door where he hesitated and turned once more to look at the younger man.

'Find Jack Fraser and kill him. And destroy that letter.'

And then he was gone.

The younger man's fragile layer of bravado collapsed as soon as the door slammed shut. He had been leaning against the wall and he slid down to the floor. Sitting there, his head in his hands, he wept, his shoulders shaking with convulsive sobs observed only by the unfeeling furniture of the room.

It was blackmail and his choice was stark. Become a traitor or have his secret life revealed to all. He closed his eyes, imagining the reaction of his father, a man of wealth and standing. There was no doubt that his father – his whole family - would reject him out of hand and cut off his inheritance.

How sudden it had been, his recruitment to the enemy side. How could he have let himself become tricked into it by this unscrupulous man who had lured him into his trap.

At length he rose to his feet, wiped his eyes and walked unsteadily to the door. He opened it and shut it behind him quietly before going out into the street.

The oil lamps in the passageway outside the building were still lit and the wind was up. The Autumn leaves were being blown from the branches and swirling around the street, lit up briefly as they passed through the arc of light. But the man did not notice them as he made his way home. The only image in his head was that of the gallows - and he'd witnessed enough hangings to know that it was not an easy end. He'd seen the poor wretches twitching and gasping in agony as onlookers jeered.

He shuddered. That would be his fate – or worse – if he did not carry out this assignment.

Chapter Eight

Neither Will nor Armstrong had had much sleep when they met up very early the next morning. Their first rendezvous was with Montagu's servant who was waiting for them in a hackney at a spot at the far edge of Seven Dials. They were then driven to the Golden Cross coaching Inn at Charing Cross in time to get the early coach to Hastings on the South coast. When they reached the large inn with its extensive stabling, it was already a bustle of activity with coaches lumbering out of the yard and passengers waiting to board. The guard dogs, the pack of Dalmatians, were still barking at every newcomer while their handler was rounding them up to put them back in their kennels.

Silently, Montagu's man handed Will a bulky sacking package then, having dismissed the hackney, he waited with them until they were safely on board the coach.

'No doubt he's been instructed to ensure we don't abscond with his master's money and arms,' whispered Armstrong. Will didn't reply but when the driver of the coach suggested that he put his package with the other luggage, Will politely refused and kept it within his sight.

Before long they had crossed the Thames and were heading South. The roads were not as rough as they had expected but the coach was a heavy vehicle pulled by four horses and their progress was slow as it lurched from side to side. Sometimes, when they came to a steep hill, the passengers had to alight and walk to the top before boarding once more. Will had hoped to be allowed to keep his own counsel and not draw attention to himself, but their fellow travellers were a talkative group and when they discovered that Will and Armstrong had never been to the South coast before, they were at pains to give them a running commentary on its charms.

'Of course, at this time of year it is not the season for visitors but oh, you should see the beaches in the summer when folk flock there to enjoy the water and all the social events. There are bathing machines and plenty of entertainments what with the military being stationed there.'

'Is it still heavily defended?' asked Will, although he already knew the answer.

'Not so much as when the threat of invasion was at its height,' said one of the gentlemen, 'but there are still barracks there and of course the Martello Towers on the coastline give people much reassurance.'

As the journey continued, the chatter was more sporadic and most of the passengers lapsed into silence or closed their eyes and tried to sleep, but there was one lady who seemed inexhaustible.

'I have been taking this journey for some years to visit my dear sister and her family and I must say that the roads have improved considerably. Why, it used to take two days to reach Hastings but now we do the journey in one. Such a relief not to have to put up in a coaching inn overnight, to say nothing of the extra expense.'

Armstrong was, by this time, asleep – or feigning it – but out of politeness, Will continued to listen, gleaning what useful information he could about the town.

They stopped once at a coaching inn to change horses and for the passengers to take some refreshment and relieve themselves. Will made discreet enquiries about where they should stay in Hastings and The Stag Inn on All Saints Street was recommended to him. Then they were on their way again and by evening they had reached their destination.

It was dark by the time they came into Hastings and the lanterns on the coach had been lit, but they could just make out the shape of the towering cliffs above the town. Will drew Armstrong's attention to them and they exchanged a glance, both men thinking how there would, no doubt, be many ancient caves in the sandstone where contraband could be concealed.

They came to a halt at the Swan coaching Inn where all the passengers disembarked.

'I'm glad we're not to lodge here,' whispered Armstrong. 'It looks too grand for the likes of us.'

Will nodded. 'No, I fancy the folk we want to meet won't be drinking their ale here.'

Taking their scant luggage and the package from Montagu, they were directed to nearby All Saints Street where they found the Stag Inn. It was an old building, recently refaced, and stood high above the pavement, the two front doors reached by stone steps on either side.

They climbed wearily up the steps and went inside to ask for accommodation. They were greeted civilly enough and given a room at the top of the building, beamed and low ceilinged, but clean and adequately furnished. The first thing that Will did was to unpack the sack containing goods from Montagu. Armstrong watched as he drew out a sword and a pistol and another bagful of coin. Will unsheathed the sword and felt the blade. Then he tested its weight and swung it from side to side.

'It is well made and short. Easily concealed.'

'You'll feel like an officer again sir.'

Will sighed. 'I'll never be that, but I shall indeed feel more comfortable if I am forced to defend myself. And you have your dagger, Sergeant.'

'Aye. Though I need more practice to use it in my left hand.'

In due course they made their way downstairs again in search of food and drink. No one took notice of them as they entered the main room. Groups sat on wooden benches crowded round tables, drinking and smoking. The conversation was loud and an occasional burst of laughter came from a corner table where a man seemed to be telling a tale to his companions who were all leaning forward to hear. At a glance, it was obvious that many of the customers were fishermen, men of the sea, with their weathered faces and gnarled hands.

'We were well advised, Sergeant,' whispered Will. 'I'd wager that many of these men supplement their income by dabbling in the smuggling trade.'

'Shall you approach them, sir?'

Will shook his head. 'Not tonight. Let's get a feel for the place tomorrow, then get into conversation with the fishermen and drop a few hints. We need to tread carefully for there will undoubtedly be Revenue men abroad.'

At length they were served a meal of bread, cheese and fish which they fell upon hungrily. Will looked up once and noticed that their presence had attracted the attention of a couple of men sitting in the corner by the open fire. When Will caught the eye of one and nodded a greeting to him he looked away quickly and neither man looked in their direction again, even when Will and Armstrong rose from their table and headed out of the door.

'Did you notice those two men sitting by the fire?' asked Will as they climbed the stairs to their room.

Armstrong shook his head. 'I never looked up from my food, I was that hungry. Why, sir?'

'I am weary and no doubt imagining things,' said Will. 'I just had a feeling …'

'Yes?'

'I had a feeling that I was recognised.'

Armstrong yawned. 'They probably recognised you as a military man and wondered why you were here and not quartered at the barracks.'

'Maybe,' said Will.

But as he was drifting off to sleep, the look of surprise on the man's face came back to him and invaded his dreams. Confused dreams of fighting in the Peninsular and the smirking face of the man who had accused him which turned, of a sudden, into the face of the man by the fire.

And of another, dearly loved face, pleading with him. "Find him for me, Will, I beg you."

***

As they ventured out the next morning, Will took a deep breath of the briny air and stretched his arms above his head. 'It is good to be out of the stench and smoke of London, is it not Sergeant?'

'It seems mighty dull here,' said Armstrong looking about him.

'I suspect it is more lively in the Summer.'

A little way down the street, Will halted and looked up at a fine large house which projected out into the road making it considerably narrower.

'Ah, this is Hastings House. It was the Duke of Wellington's headquarters until two years ago,' he said.

Armstrong grunted. 'How do you come by this knowledge?'

Will smiled. 'Our talkative fellow traveller was a mine of information,' he said. 'She told me that at the height of the time when invasion was threatened, there were no less than 12,000 troops quartered here. Cavalry, Infantry, Artillery.'

'And now?'

Will shrugged. 'Many less than that since Napoleon is fully occupied in the Peninsular, but the 2nd and 14th Dragoons are still here, among others.'

There were a few folk abroad in the town, shopkeepers going about their business, a group of military men on horseback and others on foot and, on the shore, some fishermen gathered about their boats, talking or mending their nets. '

Armstrong gestured towards them. 'Shall we go to speak with them?'

Will frowned. 'I think we'll take a walk first, Sergeant.' He pointed to the steep cliff behind them.

'You wish me to climb all the way up there?'

'Humour me, Sergeant,' said Will, 'I'd like to understand the layout of the place,' and he set off at a brisk pace.

Armstrong followed, muttering curses. It was a very steep climb; his feet slipped on the turf and he found balancing difficult with only one arm. Occasionally he was forced to drop to his knees and do an ungainly crawl so as not to lose his footing. Both men were sweating heavily when, finally, they reached the top.

Although the air was sharp and there was a strong breeze blowing off the sea, the sun was shining and the view clear.

Will shaded his eyes and pointed. 'Halton Barracks are to the West of the town. That's where the troops are quartered.'

They both stared in the direction of the barracks and although they could see nothing much at this distance, they could imagine the cleaning of weapons, the discipline of the military day, the parades and the general camaraderie of being surrounded by your fellow soldiers.

'Do you miss it Sergeant?'

'Course I do. And you, sir?'

'Yes,' he said slowly. 'Despite all that has happened.' He swallowed and then said quietly, 'It was my life.'

Armstrong stamped his foot. 'It's such a bloody shame,' he shouted, his voice deadened by the wind. 'It should never have come to this.'

'No good looking back, Sergeant. Look forward. Look over there across the Channel.'

They both stared at the water beyond the sands at the edge of the town below, stretching towards the horizon, the light sparkling on the waves.

'Hard to think that such a peaceful scene should harbour such skulduggery beneath its surface.'

Armstrong frowned. 'And why is it, sir, that you have dragged me all the way up here. Just to admire the view, is it?'

For answer, Will went nearer the cliff edge and lay on his stomach. 'See the coves down there? There are many little hidden bays where a fishing boat could anchor at night and offload its cargo.'

Huffing and puffing with effort, Armstrong lay down beside him and followed his gaze. 'Aye, and no doubt there are caves in those cliffs behind the coves.'

'I suspect there's a whole network of caves. Caves going deep inside the cliff where goods can be stored.'

'They risk much, these smugglers,' said Armstrong.

'No doubt they think the rewards worth the risk. And I suspect there are many who reach some sort of accommodation with the Preventives and allow them a few barrels of spirits and other goods in return for turning a blind eye.'

Armstrong struggled to his feet. 'That's all well and good, sir, but how is this going to help you find your brother?'

Will sighed. 'In truth, I have no idea, but if Jack has been asking questions here, then for sure someone will know about it. It is my belief that most fishing families living here are involved in smuggling in some way and news travels fast.'

'Huh. So we kick our heels and wait, do we?'

'Someone may know something. Even if not here, then in other communities along the coast. And someone may mistake me for Jack.'

Armstrong did not look convinced. 'And what if they do not?'

'Then we shall have to think again.'

When they had descended the cliff, Armstrong suggested going to see if they could find the entrance to some of the caves by walking round from the town beach.

'That would not be practical,' said Will, laughing.

'Why? It would be good to explore them would it not?'

'Not unless you are a strong swimmer.'

'What? You know I cannot swim.'

'The caves are only accessible by boat and then only at low tide. That is what makes them perfect for the smugglers.'

'Huh, the sea's a mystery to me. It nearly did for me in the Bay of Biscay. I've never trusted it.'

As they were walking back to the main part of the town, they heard a heated exchange between a group of folk in front of them. Two families were standing in the middle of the path flinging accusations at each other. There were two men, two women and a gaggle of frightened children. The adults were so engrossed in their quarrel that Will and Armstrong were able to overhear some of their shouts.

'We had a deal,' said one of the men, poking his finger into the chest of the other as his wife tried to pull him back. 'I put in the work and took the risk. I take the bulk of the winnings.'

'There was no such deal,' shouted the other. He turned to his wife. 'You heard nothing of this, Meg, did you?'

'Course not. He's trying it on.' Then she faced up to the first man, her arms folded. 'You're naught but a swindling bastard, Tom Little, even if you are my cousin.'

Suddenly the group became aware that they had company and they fell silent as Will and Armstrong passed by.

'Those two men were in the tavern last night,' said Will in an undertone. 'They were sitting by the fire.'

'Was one of them the man you fancied recognised you?'

'Aye,' said Will. 'But I was tired and seeing danger in every corner. It was nothing but a result of a fevered imagination for neither man noted me just now.'

They spent the rest of the morning acquainting themselves with the town, making conversation with shopkeepers and passing the time of day with some of the fishermen as they readied their boats to go out into the water again. Armstrong became more and more restless.

'You may find all this idling about very pleasant, sir, but I can't for the life of me see the point of it.'

Will shrugged. 'There may be no point to it my friend, but if Jack was here, I'll warrant someone will take note of our presence and may think he's here again.'

'Huh! It's naught but a wild goose chase.'

Privately, Will was thinking the same thing and wondering what his next step should be but he resolved at least to send a message to Montagu by the next mail coach even though there was nothing of note to report.

Armstrong announced that he would walk to the barracks at Halton and see if he could glean any useful information. Will nodded his agreement though he knew it was merely an excuse to get into conversation with soldiers, those of his ilk who he missed so sorely.

'Be sure to be back at the Stag before sunset,' he said, then he turned his attention to the laborious task of writing a message in the complicated code that Montagu had devised.

It seems hardly necessary if I'm just to convey to him that we have arrived in Hastings.

By the time this was done, the afternoon was drawing to a close. Will took the letter and set off down the street to walk to the Swan coaching inn.

The shadows were lengthening as he walked back having made his delivery and he was deep in thought when he suddenly heard his name called out.

'Fraser!'

Will whipped round, his hand going immediately to his sword, but he could see no one and he stood, alert, staring into the gloom. Then a man emerged suddenly, as if from nowhere, and grabbed his sword arm.

'What in God's name are you doing here?'

Will made no answer but he recognised the man from the morning's encounter and from last night in the Stag.

He does recognise me!

The man did not release Will's arm but continued in a low tone. 'You told me that secrecy was vital, man, yet here you are, strolling about the town in plain sight. What is going on and how, in God's name, did you return from France with such speed when we only conveyed you there a few days ago?'

Chapter Nine

London

Clara Fraser was not a woman who was usually prone to tears, indeed she prided herself on being level-headed and sensible, not the hysterical or swooning type.

She was a girl from the North who had lived on her father's estate, had ridden his horses and had had more education than most from the governesses he had employed to teach her. At first she had been somewhat overwhelmed by the life to which she had been introduced by Jack and often found the social events and the town gossip excruciatingly boring. But she was gradually finding her feet in London and was beginning to make friendships with women like her who took an interest in subjects beyond the fashions and scandals of the day.

Jack had guided her with his easy charm and his sharp intellect and introduced her to those with whom he knew she would have something in common; lately she had begun to settle and have a measure of confidence in the glittering London life on whose periphery they lived. And she took pleasure, too, in making their apartment in Lincoln's Inn into a home, softening the austere furnishings with touches of femininity and making sure that the cook they had employed knew how to serve Jack's favourite food.

Now, however, that self-confidence was ebbing away. Although she put on a brave face and told her new acquaintances that Jack was away on Government business, she was finding it increasingly hard to keep up the pretence that she knew where he was or what was happening to him.

In private, she shed tears and prayed fervently for his safe return, but she was bewildered by the complete silence surrounding his disappearance. Surely, he could have told her that he was going away? They trusted one another completely and he had sworn to her that he would always be in communication, wherever he was, that, somehow, he would get word to her. But it had been over ten days since he had disappeared so suddenly and there had been no word from him – or of him – so, it was with a mixture of eagerness and trepidation that she heard her maid announce that James Montagu had come to call on her.

As always, Montagu was dressed immaculately and he strode into the room, smiling and looking about him. He took her hand and kissed it and complimented her on the changes she had made to the décor.

Clara wasted no time on an exchange of pleasantries and came straight to the point.

'Is there any news of Jack?"

Montagu held up his hands. 'Alas, my dear, I still know nothing of his whereabouts, but his brother is searching diligently for him and I have high hopes that he will track Jack down.'

'You have high hopes? Is Will under instruction from you, then? From the Government?'

'Not exactly.' Montagu busied himself flicking a tiny speck of dirt from his coat, then continued. 'He has been supplied with money and arms and, of course, with his close relationship to Jack, he is as eager as you and I to find him.'

Clara sat down suddenly and looked up at Montagu. 'I do not understand.'

Montagu remained standing and Clara could tell that he was debating how much to disclose of his plans.

'You know that I am discreet, sir,' she said quietly.

Montagu nodded. 'Of that I have no doubt,' he replied. 'But I am not in a position to tell you more.' He was silent for a moment and then continued. 'There is a delicate task ahead of us, Clara, and for the moment Jack can trust no one which is why, I am sure, he has remained out of communication. I suspect he feels it is safer this way.'

'But not to contact me! I am his wife!'

'I'm sorry that he has left you in ignorance, but I am sure he has his reasons. Above all he will be anxious to keep you out of danger.'

'Yes,' said Clara slowly 'I am aware that his work can be dangerous. That was amply demonstrated by the attack on Will, was it not?'

'Captain Fraser is a soldier and a fine swordsman.'

'Captain Fraser? I thought …'

'A slip of the tongue.'

'So you are saying that if Will is mistaken for Jack, he would have a better chance of defending himself?'

'You are very astute, my dear.'

'But I still do not understand Will's involvement. Surely there are others better suited …'

Montagu's expression hardened. 'No more questions, Clara. I am here to do my best to reassure you and beg you not to worry but there are some things I cannot share with you.'

Clara, however, continued to try and find out more but Montagu, with consummate skill, refused to be drawn and turned the conversation to safer topics asking after the health of Clara's family in the North and her plans for diversion in London during the Winter months, but just before he left, he took both her hands in his.

'It is important, my dear, that you do not fret. Honour any social obligations you have, act normally, and if anyone asks after Jack, simply say that he is away on Government business.'

'And if I should be pressed further?'

'Then say that you do not bother yourself with such matters and act as though you are an empty-headed young woman enjoying all the pleasures that London has to offer.'

'What!'

James Montagu laughed. 'You can act empty headed for once, Clara, can you not?'

Clara scowled at him.

He left shortly afterwards and she walked over to the window and watched him leave the building, get into his phaeton and drive away. For some minutes she stood there, her brow furrowed. Although she had sometimes questioned Jack about his work, he had told her little except that he was employed by the Government and that the nature of the job meant that he was unable to discuss it with her. She had had to accept this but nonetheless she had made her own assumptions and guessed, correctly, that he was involved in some form of intelligence gathering.

She had been unnerved by Montagu's visit. He knew that Jack and she were close. Had he come to ascertain whether she was truly in ignorance? Did he suspect that Jack had confided in her and that she, too, was playing a game of deception?

Montagu is ill at ease and afraid, however confident and urbane he may seem. He and Jack have been working together so closely but now it is obvious that he has no idea what has happened to him or where he is.

She paced around the room, no longer taking delight in its welcoming atmosphere or in the furnishings she had so carefully arranged, and scarcely replying when her maid entered and asked if she needed any refreshment.

She was thinking back to happier times, to all that she and Jack had shared, not just during their short marriage but during their childhoods when the delight they found in each other's company was uncomplicated. From an early age they had shared so much – a love of nature, of stories, of puzzles and the unravelling of mysteries. Jack had often set her conundrums and riddles as she had done for him and they had vied with one another to solve them. She stopped pacing and began to chew at her finger, a habit from childhood which she had never broken and did, without thinking, whenever she was agitated.

Think, Clara, think! Jack had to leave very suddenly. If he'd had time to do so he would have let me know where he was going, would he not? Or at least that he was going. But he had no time, he was fleeing for his life, and it sounds as though he could trust no one to get a message to me, fearing that it would be intercepted. But he, above all, knows my nature and my skill at solving puzzles. He would know that I would worry away at this, the most baffling of puzzles.

She remembered, then, a conversation she and Jack had had not long after their marriage when Jack had suddenly taken her in his arms and told her that she must always trust him. At the time she had laughed at him and said that of course she would, but he had not joined in her laughter and instead had stroked her hair, loosed his clasp and held her a little away from him.

'My love, sometimes my work may put me in danger. I may sometimes have to go away but I swear to you, on my word of honour, that I will always, one way or another, keep you informed of my whereabouts. Will you swear to me, on your part, that you will never doubt me?'

He had looked so serious that she became serious, too, and put up a hand to stroke his cheek.

'I have never doubted you for one moment, and I never shall,' she had said. 'I would trust you with my life.'

Tears were gathering in her eyes as she remembered this conversation but she wiped them away with the back of her hand. Something had struck her about his exact words.

One way or another.

Could he have used another method to leave her a message. But what? And how? She imagined him in his rented room at Mrs Baxter's lodging house, frantically throwing his possessions together, trusting no one, with no time to get a note to her, no time to do anything except flee from those who wanted to harm him. Could he possibly have left her a note concealed somewhere in that room, written in their silly secret code?

A fanciful idea but perhaps worth pursuing?

I cannot sit here and wait for news and nor can I pretend no concern. And I certainly cannot bear to attend tedious social events. I must do something.

She stood quite still, thinking how she could gain access to the room that Jack had vacated and then, of a sudden it came to her and she allowed herself a faint smile. Rummaging in the drawer where they kept their household papers, she extracted a receipt, then hastily donned her cloak, bonnet and veil and called to her maid that she was going out.

Chapter Ten

London

James Montagu was ill at ease. He had been summoned to attend on John Reeves, head of the Alien Office, to give an account of himself. Although officially a part of the Home Office, the Alien Office was not situated in Whitehall but in Crown Street in Westminster, and as Montagu drove away from Lincoln's Inn, he rehearsed in his mind what he would say to Reeves, a legal man with a keen intelligence who had held several important roles at home and abroad and was known to be a fierce anti-republican. He was a man who did not suffer fools gladly and would demand an explanation of Montagu's recent conduct.

Montagu was ushered inside the building and asked to wait in the lobby. There was a tall grandfather clock in the corner and as he sat on an upright chair, one of many ranged along the wall opposite the clock, he watched the minutes tick by and listened to the chime of the hour.

Is this waiting necessary? Or is it to unnerve me?

At length, a clerk came to fetch him and he was taken up some stairs and into a room lined with books. A fire was burning merrily in the grate and John Reeves was sitting behind a desk cluttered with papers and scrolls. At Montagu's entrance he stood up and leant over the desk to shake his hand then sat down again. He did not suggest that Montagu sit but came immediately to the point.

'So, James, you have lost Jack Fraser?'

Montagu expressed no surprise that Reeves was privy to this information. He had informants all over the city and, indeed, all over the country and beyond. Although James and Jack were close to the centre of the gathering of intelligence, the network of spies, by its very nature was far reaching and secretive.

'Not exactly, sir.'

'How not exactly? The information seems very precise. Jack Fraser has gone missing has he not, there is no word from him and now you have concocted this hare-brained scheme of setting his disgraced brother on his trail.'

James tried not to betray his shock. The idea of asking Will Fraser to look for his brother had been his alone and it had been taken on the spur of the moment, after he had first met Will. He had not shared it with colleagues.

'It seemed an opportunity not to be missed, sir.'

'Why?'

Montagu swallowed. 'Because of their close resemblance, sir.'

Reeves stared at him. 'And how exactly would this help our cause?'

Montagu looked towards the door as if expecting there to be someone listening at the keyhole. Reeves drummed his fingers on the surface of the desk.

'Jack Fraser may have vital information, sir. He hinted to me, just before he disappeared, that he had made a discovery which might lead to the identity of the high-ranking person who has unmasked our agents and destroyed all that we have been working towards these last months.'

'What do you mean by a high-ranking person?'

Montagu licked his lips. 'Possibly a member of the Government,' he said.

Montagu had expected Reeves to deny this as preposterous but the man's face remained expressionless.

'And you thought that the life of a disgraced ex-soldier was of no value but that he might be mistaken for Jack and killed so the attackers think they have dispatched Jack and put an end to his line of enquiry?'

'Not exactly sir, more … more as a decoy to confuse our enemies.'

The more he spoke of it, the more unlikely the plan seemed, even to his own ears.

'And how do you know, Montagu, that Jack Fraser has not taken others into his confidence?'

Montagu cleared his throat. 'I cannot be sure, sir, but as you know, he and I work in close collaboration and I would have expected him to share this confidence with me, above all others, yet he gave me no name or other details – and he disappeared without warning.'

Reeves reached for the snuff box on his desk, opened the lid, took out a goodly pinch and put it on the back of his hand, from whence he transferred it, first to one nostril and then the other, sniffing it up loudly.

'I am not happy that Jack seems to have acted alone on this; it is against protocol, as you know. But it is essential that we catch this traitor, Montagu. Through his actions he has destroyed months of planning and identified agents who will now be unable to work for us again as their names are known to the enemy. At one stroke he has unravelled almost our entire intelligence operation in Northern France.'

Suddenly he jumped to his feet, the snuff box flying, its contents spilling all over the desk.

'Good God, it is infuriating! All these months of planning, all the secret communications, the care we have taken at every stage. This operation could have made a real difference to the war. Do you know how much planning was involved, Montagu? Even you and Jack were not privy to every detail, nor, indeed, were our agents. They only knew what they had to do and when. I have racked my brain but there is no-one. No-one to whom I can point the finger, no-one who knew enough to bring down so much of our network to such devastating effect. I would trust with my life all those who knew the whole breadth of it. Who in heaven's name can it be?'

Montagu had never seen Reeves so angry and it unsettled him. 'I know that only very few knew the full details of the operation, sir, and the very fact that Jack apparently trusts no one, that he disappeared with such haste from his lodgings leads me to think that you are right to think that he has good reason to fear for his safety.' He hesitated, then continued. 'There has been an incident which bears this out.'

'Oh?'

Montagu had not meant to mention the attack on Will but he could see that this might strengthen his case for doing what he had done.

'There was an attack on his brother, sir. Will Fraser arrived very recently back from Portugal and sought Jack out only to find he had left his lodgings in apparent haste. While Will Fraser was in Drury Lane he was viciously attacked by some villains. They apprehended him and called out his name.'

Reeves had clearly not had this particular piece of information relayed to him. He frowned. 'What happened?'

'They ran away when he fought them off.' He hesitated. They may have realised that they had the wrong man.' He shrugged. 'Or they may have not fancied grappling further with a skilled fighter.'

'Then the resemblance to his brother is not so marked if you say they may have realised they had the wrong man?'

'I am hoping that he has done as I asked and made it more so.'

There was a long silence while Reeves paced up and down the room, his hands clasped behind his back.

'And where is he now, this disgraced soldier?' he said at last.

'He is on the South coast, with his Sergeant.'

'His Sergeant? I was told that Will Fraser was thrown out of his regiment.'

'While saving his Sergeant's life, I believe,' said Montagu.

'Hmm,' said Reeves. 'And what are they doing on the South coast?'

'It is only surmise, sir, but as you know, documents outlining details of the operation and identifying our agents were copied and fell into enemy hands. We found them in the possession of one of the French spies but he escaped our clutches before we could force from him the name of the person who supplied them.'

Montagu took a silk handkerchief from his pocket and wiped his brow. 'It is my belief, sir, that our traitor may have used a smuggler to convey these documents over to our enemies, or even taken them himself. I think Jack may be on his trail and if that is the case then our traitor will do everything to ensure Jack is silenced. Only then will he be able to continue to undermine our intelligence network, operating here as a trusted servant of our Government. The man will do anything to keep his name secret. We have no idea of Jack Fraser's whereabouts but my guess is that he may have gone to France.'

'On this whim of yours, then, our disgraced soldier and his Sergeant have travelled to the South coast, eh?'

Montagu fiddled with the cloth at his neck which, of a sudden, seemed too tight.

'If Jack is hiding in France and Will Fraser poses as his brother,' he said quietly, 'then we could perhaps flush out our traitor.'

'And how would that occur?'

Montagu knew he would be asked this question.

'A fair question, sir.'

Reeves raised an eyebrow.

Montagu chose his words carefully. He needed to convince Reeves that his action was valid.

'Will Fraser has a code to use when he communicates with me. A new code which has not been used before. He will alert me immediately he discovers anything. This is such a dire betrayal that it is understandable that Jack trusts no one, not even his closest colleagues nor our agents, but if Will finds Jack, then Jack will certainly trust him to convey any information back to us so that we can take action.'

Reeves began to sweep the spilled snuff on the desk into his hand and trickle it back into the snuff box. He said nothing.

Montagu shifted his feet slightly. 'I realise this is unorthodox, sir, but I trust Will Fraser. Before this recent business with his regiment, I understand that he was well thought of by his men and fellow officers alike. He has fought bravely for his country and is no coward.'

'Hmm. I had heard that he was accused of cowardice.'

'I think that bears investigation, sir.'

'Well, that is a military matter and no concern of ours. As you know, many of our operatives in the field come from dubious backgrounds.

Montagu gave a thin smile. He and Jack had encountered many informants of dubious reputation and Jack had a nose for sorting out the nuggets of real gold from the dross which was passed to them.

Reeves then lapsed into another of his long silences. Although Montagu did his best to conceal his agitation, he could feel the sweat trickling down his back as he waited for the verdict.

At last Reeves sighed deeply. 'I hardly need to tell you why the capture of this traitor is so important, Montagu. If he is not identified and continues to be trusted as one of ours, then nothing we pass to our agents will be safe. Nothing.'

Montagu nodded. 'If Jack Fraser is truly on his trail, I know he will do everything in his power to stop him conveying more intelligence to the other side.

'Silencing him permanently, you mean? I don't see Jack as a killer.

'No,' said Montagu slowly. 'But his brother is.'

'And you really think Will Fraser could be instrumental in achieving this?'

'Sir, I cannot be sure, but what is certain is his love for Jack. He is as eager to find him as we are. Will knows that he will be exposing himself to danger but he's a skilled soldier and can look after himself.'

Another long silence. Then 'Very well, Montagu, but I will need to be kept informed of any developments.'

Montagu's shoulders untensed. 'Of course, sir.'

'Immediately.'

'Immediately, sir.'

Chapter Eleven

Hastings

For a few moments, Will was dumbfounded by the fisherman's statement but he quickly gathered his wits.

'Ye gods, man, you startled me!'

The fisherman laughed. 'And you me, sir! At first I thought I was seeing a ghost who had flitted back across the channel by some mystic means! And you were hiding yourself away when we last met but now you're in plain sight, in the tavern and strolling along the cliff path like you want the world to see you.'

Frantically, Will searched his memory for the man's name. He'd heard it on the path, the woman Meg had mentioned it. Tom, that was it.

'You're right, Tom. On that first voyage, I was anxious that none saw me leave, but this time it's different.'

Tom rubbed the side of his nose with his finger. 'Say no more, sir. It's none of my business. We ask no questions in my line of work. Will you be wanting my services again, sir?'

Will was thinking fast *I must tread carefully so as not to raise his suspicions but if I can find out where he took Jack, it will be a beginning.*

He nodded. 'Can you convey me to the same place again?'

'Near to Gravelines?'

'Aye, to Gravelines.'

Tom grinned. 'That's a good choice, sir. They say Napoleon's minded to make it a base for English smugglers, make it easier for the likes of us to ply our trade. Even now the guards there mostly turn a blind eye if we slip them a little sweetener.

Will nodded as if he was already privy to this information. 'How soon can you take me?'

Tom frowned. 'Well …' He rubbed his chin. 'It could be as soon as tomorrow, sir. We have some business happening tomorrow night when we're meeting up with a galley going across.'

'A galley? Then you won't make the crossing yourself?'

'Not this time, sir, so it should be a deal more comfortable for you than when I took you before.'

'And this galley?'

'Coming down from Dover.'

'And who will be on board?'

'The Master's a good seaman. That's all you need to know.'

Will smiled. 'I'm not asking you to betray confidences, Tom. I just need to know whether the crew will be willing to take me and if they are discreet.'

Tom chuckled. 'Discreet! They'll be as silent as the grave. They take all sorts across and collect all sorts to bring them back. Never ask no questions.'

'Not only goods?'

'Nah! Spies, escaped prisoners of war. The Master's not fussy so long as he gets paid.' Tom frowned. 'But he won't accept nothing but specie in payment sir. Do you have coin?'

Will nodded, thankful that the money given him by Montagu was all in coin. Little of it was made of base metal, either. He had plenty of silver and a supply of gold half guineas, too. He suspected that the Master of this vessel would charge highly and, no doubt, the resourceful Tom would demand a considerable percentage for making the arrangements.

'I shall have a companion with me, Tom.'

Tom frowned. 'You said last time you were operating on your own.'

'I was, but there's been a … development. And I can assure you that my companion is utterly to be trusted. He has no interest in your activities.'

Tom stroked his chin. 'Even so …'

Will sighed. 'I'll pay you well. And the Master of the galley. And Tom …'

How shall I phrase this. Getting across the Channel is one thing but I have no idea where Jack went then.

'Yes sir?'

'Once across the Channel …?'

Tom frowned and looked at Will questioningly then he shrugged. 'No doubt you'll be met as before. There's always someone on lookout.'

They agreed on a price and a time to meet up the next evening and then they parted company but Will felt that the fisherman had become of a sudden less trusting and although his face was obscured by the gathering darkness, Will could sense his wariness. He swore under his breath.

Have I slipped up somehow? Did I say something which did not ring true, perhaps?

***

Shortly after Will had made his way back to the Stag Inn and was writing another brief dispatch for Montagu to tell him of his meeting with the fisherman, Armstrong came back. The Sergeant was in high spirits and he crashed through the door, staggering slightly.

'My God, sir, it was good to be among the military again!'

'No doubt,' said Will, not looking up. He was struggling with the code as he tried to convey this extra news in the shortest way possible.'

'Let me tell you …'began Armstrong.

'Not now, Sergeant. I have an urgent note to send to Montagu and I need to concentrate, and then I'd be grateful if you could take it down to the Swan and pay for it to be dispatched with the night mail coach to London.'

Armstrong walked over to the window and looked out into the darkness. Pinpricks of light were visible where lanterns were lit in the buildings in All Saints Street but no one was abroad. He drummed his fingers on the windowsill and began to hum a ditty he had picked up in the tavern at the barracks.

'Hush man, let me think!'

'Sorry sir.'

At last the dispatch was finished and sealed and Armstrong lumbered out of the room and down the stairs. Will heard the front door slam behind him and a curse as the Sergeant had apparently stumbled down the steep steps onto the street.

Will lay down on his bed and laced his hands behind his head. He smiled. He could not be vexed with Armstrong for long. The man deserved some diversion and interaction with his own and who knows, he might even have discovered some useful information.

When Armstrong returned, Will listened patiently to his account of all he had seen and heard at the barracks, mostly at the tavern there which was apparently frequented almost exclusively by the soldiery. He recounted anecdotes about the officers in charge, the soldiers' complaints about the lack of entertainment during the coming Winter months and intelligence about the war. Mostly, Will only listened with half an ear but when Armstrong mentioned that the British forces had a few days ago entered Spain, he was all attention.

'Aye,' said Armstrong. 'Bonaparte's brother may have been appointed King of Spain in August but he was only there a few days before he had to flee.'

'I know that, Sergeant. The Spanish insurgents rose up against him.'

'And now,' said Armstrong, 'it is rumoured that the Emperor himself is planning to leave France and join his forces in Spain within the week.'

'We should not put much store by rumours, Sergeant.'

Montagu and his network will know of this. They will have spies in Spain no doubt, in league with the insurgents. Will the traitor have uncovered their plans there, too?

When Armstrong had finally finished the account of his time at the barracks, Will got up from his bed and stretched.

'And now, Sergeant, let me tell you my news. 'We are to sail over to France tomorrow night.'

Armstrong stared at him. 'What! You're not asking me to get on another bloody boat, sir?'

Will laughed. 'It's the only way to get there, Sergeant.'

Then he proceeded to relay to Armstrong his meeting with Tom and how he had discovered that the fisherman had taken Jack to France only days since.

'Tom seemed convinced that I was Jack, so the disguise works well.'

'Those young actresses knew what they were about,' said Armstrong.

'So it would seem.'

They were silent for a while and Will sensed that Armstrong was wondering whether they would ever cross paths with Sally and Lottie again.

'Come,' said Will. Let's go and take some supper downstairs.'

As they were eating, Armstrong suddenly looked up. 'Your friends aren't in tonight.'

Will looked round the room. There was no sign of Tom or his companion.

'No doubt busying themselves with preparations for tomorrow.'

Armstrong nodded, then turned back to his food and took another mouthful. 'You were wrong about the caves, sir,' he said, his words indistinct.

'Oh?'

'The main entrances aren't from the sea, they're from above, from the cliff. Like a honeycomb it is, apparently, with a whole network of caverns. My soldier pals tell me they meet there sometimes to play cards and gamble.'

'Well well, Sergeant. A good place to keep things dry and hidden then, but the smugglers must have a way of conveying their ill-gotten gains from their boats to these caves, surely?'

'No doubt we'll find out.'

They continued their meal in companionable silence and when they had finished, Armstrong puffed away at a clay pipe, Will having helped him to pack the bowl with shredded tobacco.

'Thanks for the extra hand, sir,' said Armstrong.

'I admire your stoicism Sergeant. You seldom complain about the injury.'

Armstrong said nothing for a while but Will knew there was something on his mind.

'Is there anything else you want to tell me?'

Armstrong took another puff. 'Only something you'll not want to hear.'

'Better spit it out.'

'You know the Northumberland Militia is billeted at the barracks – the Buffs, they call them?'

'Yes, they're a long way from home. Tom told me that they're here now on anti- smuggling duties, but he didn't seem to rate them very highly. They aren't a regular fighting force, just a militia of volunteers raised to help in times of war.'

'Aye. And do you know the name of their Colonel?'

Will frowned. 'No idea, but it will be some gentleman with a deal of money and land, no doubt.'

'That's about right, sir,' said Armstrong, slowly. Then he looked Will in the eye and told him the name.

Will felt the familiar stab of misery which had been with him ever since he realised that he would lose his commission and be drummed out of the army in disgrace. For the last few days he'd been less troubled by it, been able to apply himself to this new task and had regained a measure of self-respect, but now it came back with a force so strong that he felt as though he'd been physically kicked in the stomach.

He swallowed. 'Is he related …?'

Armstrong nodded. 'He's the bastard's father.'

'Well,' said Will at last. 'I doubt our paths will cross, but thank you for telling me.'

'Thought you should know, sir, in case you want to go over to Halton and run the man through with your sword.'

Will gave a wan smile and scraped his chair back from the table. 'We should get some sleep,' he muttered.

Chapter Twelve

London

Clara pounded on Mrs Baxter's door with a force induced by all the frustration and impotence she felt after Montagu's visit.

At first there was no activity from within but, when Clara pounded again, there was the sound of feet approaching with no apparent hurry, no urgent response to the force of the knocking.

Mrs Baxter opened the door herself, an insolent smirk on her face. She didn't invite Clara in but stood looking her up and down.

'What do you want?'

Clara was in no mood to prevaricate. 'A civil greeting for a start,' she said, pushing herself past the woman and into the house.

'Hey, what do you think you are doing, Madame? This is my house and I'll thank you to leave it this instant.'

Clara's eyes narrowed. 'I am Jack Fraser's wife and I demand to be given access to his room.'

Mrs Baxter folded her arms across her chest and tilted her chin at Clara.

'Huh, you say you are his wife. I've no proof of that.'

Clara's colour heightened. 'I refuse to dignify that comment with a reply.'

Mrs Baxter said nothing but just raised an eyebrow.

Clara reached into the pocket of her cloak and brought out a piece of paper. At the sight of it, the other woman's expression changed and became wary.

'Here I have the receipt you signed, Mrs Baxter, for my husband's rental of that room until the end of this month.' Clara waved the paper at her. 'Yet I know you have already charged my brother-in-law for a night in it and I have absolutely no doubt that you have rented it again to someone else even though the month is not yet expired.'

Mrs Baxter took a step back. 'But Mr Fraser emptied it. Cleared out without notice. What did you expect me to do?'

'Had you an arrangement that if he left before the month was up, you could re-let it?'

'Well no, but I …'

'Then legally he still has occupancy.'

The word legal seemed to unbalance Mrs Baxter. She put one hand on the table behind her and the other to her chest.

'I'm just a poor widow trying to make a living, Madame,' she said. 'I do my best for my lodgers and they are very satisfied with the service I provide.'

'No doubt,' said Clara. 'Now please take me to Mr Fraser's room.'

'But it's …'

'I do not care if there is another lodger there, Mrs Baxter. I wish to see the room.'

Grudgingly, Mrs Baxter led Clara up the stairs. 'The gentleman is out at present but I'll thank you not to disturb his possessions,' she said, as she opened the door.

'I have no intention of disturbing anything, Mrs Baxter,' said Clara as she walked into the room. 'Now please leave me alone. I may be some time.' Then she shut the door firmly in Mrs Baxter's face and leant her back against it, observing the room and waiting to regain her composure.

Truly I have no idea why I am here, Jack, but I cannot believe that you left no clue behind, no hint of why you disappeared so suddenly. I understand that you had no time to alert anyone, even me, and that you were fearful for your life. But we have always been honest with one another.

Clara raised her head and looked up at the ceiling for inspiration. 'Dear Lord,' she muttered, 'Protect him from harm I beg you.'

Then she sat down at the desk which was under the window and opened the lid. She had no real hope of finding anything of significance but somehow the very thought that Jack had occupied the room until only recently gave her some comfort. Will had told her that he had already searched every crevice of the place in case there was something which might throw light on the reason for Jack's sudden disappearance, but Clara, just to satisfy herself, decided to do her own examination thoroughly and methodically.

Before she began, however, she thought of all the intimacies that she and Jack had shared.

Is there something that might make sense only to me, perhaps? A message in some sort of code which only I could decipher? Or could Jack have left something here, well hidden, to give Montagu an idea of where he's gone? But surely that is fanciful?

Clara frowned. She had received very few letters in the last couple of weeks though she was herself an avid correspondent, writing to her family and friends in the North describing the goings on in the capital.

Have my own letters been intercepted – or read before they reach their destination I wonder? Surely they are of no interest to Jack's enemies? How could they be?

But that seed of doubt being sown, Clara thought back to an incident a few days ago when a letter from a friend had arrived with its seal broken. Her servant had said that the boy who delivered it was tearful and apologetic and said he had had a fall on his way. Clara had thought no more about the incident. Until now.

She was unimpressed by the habits of the room's current occupant, whoever he was. There was rubbish on the floor, clothes strewn everywhere, soiled undergarments stuffed into a drawer, a pair of boots kicked carelessly under the bed and nothing hung up in the closet. And a distinct smell of an unwashed and sweaty body.

Clara was not squeamish, however. She picked up every garment, opened every drawer, looked behind the mirror and the few pictures which hung on the wall, behind the curtains and even tested the floorboards to see if there was one loose which might be prised up. At one point Betsy came into the room carrying a tall cup of chocolate. The girl looked round the room.

'He doesn't keep it like Mr Jack did,' she said. She put the chocolate down on a table. 'Mrs Baxter said you might like some refreshment.'

Clara smiled. 'Thank you, Betsy, that was thoughtful of her.'

It seems Mrs B is trying to make amends!

As Betsy turned to leave, Clara asked after Sally. 'Are she and her companion still here, Betsy, or have they been thrown out?'

'No, they're still here Madame. They've found a bit of work at the theatre here in the Lane.'

'I'm glad for them.'

'They'll be back soon to get ready,' said Betsy. 'Shall I send them up when they come in?'

'I'd be pleased to see them if that won't hold them up.'

'Nah, I reckon they'd like that.' She paused. 'I don't suppose there's any news of Mr Jack?'

Clara shook her head and Betsy withdrew, then Clara sat down on the chair at the desk and started to sip her chocolate. She stroked the top of the desk, the wood well worn, with marks and scratches all over. She frowned. Something about it was familiar and she looked at it more carefully. Was this the desk that Jack had had as a child? Had he brought it down from the North with him?

Strange that this is the only furniture here that belongs to him. Does that hold any significance, I wonder?

Although she had been through every drawer in the desk already, she did so once more, pulling them all out. They were all empty.

Will was right. Jack has left nothing here.

Then, as she was staring at the empty drawers, she noticed that one of the small ones at the top didn't seem to match its pair on the other side. Its back was thicker and it was shorter inside than its fellow. Carefully, she pulled at it until it came free of its runners and she held it up to examine it. She turned it this way and that, her heart beating a little faster.

Does his old childhood desk hold a secret? Jack knows my love of secrets and puzzles. Could he have left me a clue within it?

And then she found what she was looking for. The tiniest metal spring on the back face of the drawer, and when she pressed it the whole back swung open to reveal a small cavity. And inside was a scrap of paper.

Very carefully, Clara felt for it and pulled it out between her fingers. Looking round nervously, she quickly replaced the drawer, shut it and all the others and closed the desk. Then she smoothed out the paper.

She recognised Jack's hand immediately and she started to shake so violently that, at first, she was unable to read what he had written. She took some deep breaths to calm herself.

It was a silly love poem of the sort that he would scribble for her from time to time, usually with a message concealed within it with the letters which went diagonally from top to bottom of the script. Sometimes they were words of love or a joke, which made her smile, and sometimes a reference to an intimate part of her body, which made her blush.

But this was different. When she read the poem, it was obviously written in haste and without his usual literary flare and attention to meter. It was not well constructed and when she read down the diagonal, all that was revealed was a name. But it was a name she recognised. The name of a man at the heart of Government.

To be concealed like this, the name must be of vital importance but I have no idea what it signifies.

But to whom was it important? Even if others had found the scrap of paper, they would only take it at face value. Only she would know, immediately, how to look for the concealed message.

She began to perspire as she looked once more at the scrap of paper. Her hands trembled as she read the other diagonal.

F R A N C E

Does this mean that Jack is in France? Is this the name of the traitor Montagu mentioned? Can it really be him? And who can I trust with this intelligence?

Her thoughts were interrupted by the sound of the front door opening followed by some chatter and then laughter. Sally and Lottie had returned and she heard their footsteps on the stairs having obviously been directed by Betsy. She shoved the scrap of paper into her pocket. She would destroy it later as she had already committed the name to memory. Then she got up, smoothed down her dress, took a deep breath to compose herself and went to greet the girls.

'Mrs B's all of a fluster,' said Lottie, giggling. 'She doesn't like getting found out.'

Clara nodded. 'I found the receipt for the room rental,' she said. 'Jack had paid for it until the end of the month.'

'She's a sharp one,' said Sally. 'Getting double the money, eh?' She looked round the room. 'He's a pig this new tenant. He doesn't look after his stuff like Mr Jack did.'

'Did you find what you were looking for?' asked Lottie.

Clara shook her head. 'I thought there might be something, some clue to Jack's whereabouts here, but there was nothing.' The lie came easily as she touched the scrap of paper in her pocket.

'Perhaps Mr Will and Sergeant Armstrong will find him,' said Lottie, then she clapped her hand over her mouth as Sally scowled at her.

'Lottie!' she hissed.

'But she's his wife!' whispered Lottie.

Clara looked from one to the other. 'You are breaching no confidence,' she said. 'I know that Will is looking for him.'

Lottie looked relieved. 'I reckon we did a good job on his disguise,' she said. 'I dyed his hair and told him to shave off his beard and gave him some salve to lighten his skin. He can easily pass for Mr Jack now.'

Clara frowned in puzzlement.

When did this happen? And why should it have been necessary?

Aloud she said. 'Do you have any idea where Will is now?'

Lottie shook her head but Sally said nothing.

'Sally,' said Clara, 'Do you know something?'

Sally frowned and looked down at her feet. 'They brought us back here after we'd done the dyeing and that, and I did hear the Sergeant say something when they walked away.'

'Yes?'

'I might have got it wrong but I think I heard him ask Mr Will what time the Hastings coach left.'

Clara made some noncommittal comment but her thoughts were racing.

Hastings is on the South coast. Could it be that Will believes that Jack has crossed the Channel from there? France was written in the code so it would make sense.

Chapter Thirteen

Mrs Baxter, clearly desperate to be rid of Clara, had sent Betsy to find a hackney and had stood at her door to watch as Clara was conveyed back to her apartment in Lincoln's Inn.

Throughout the short journey, Clara's thoughts were in turmoil. One thing was clear to her, however. By great good fortune, she had found a name which was important enough for Jack to conceal it in a way that only she would discover it. He could not know that she would find it but he, above everyone, knew her nature. He knew that she would do everything in her power to discover what had happened to him and would probably search his room. And he knew her love of tricks and puzzles. It seemed that he had unearthed a truth about a powerful man which he could share with no-one, not even his colleagues, and disguised it in a crude love poem so that, even if discovered, it would mean nothing to anyone but her. Was that why he had vanished so abruptly, trusting no one with this secret? But what did it mean? That the man named was a traitor? Someone in league with the French? It seemed preposterous. And if this was so, what would he expect her to do with this knowledge? Something held her back from sharing it with Montagu but was there anyone else she could trust with it?

And then, of a sudden, it came to her.

Jack would have known nothing of Will's arrival in the country but Clara was absolutely certain that he would trust his brother. She had known Will since childhood and she would trust him with her life, as would Jack. If Will was still in Hastings, she would find him. If he was furnished with this intelligence, then he would be forewarned when he searched for Jack and be on his guard if any messages or instructions came from the man mentioned in the note. But if Will was planning to cross the Channel, she must find him before he left. She must go immediately and she must travel in secret.

By the time she reached her lodgings, she had formed a plan. It involved a deal of lying and deceit, but if she were being drawn into this murky world, then she determined to play by its rules.

It was frightening that the lies came so easily. She told her maid that she had met up with her brother and that they would travel North early tomorrow to visit her father, who was unwell. If anyone came to visit, then that was the story they would hear.

She then visited the stables from which she had previously hired horses to ride in the park and arranged to hire one to take her, she told them, on the first stage up North. She would be accompanied by her brother, she explained, who would meet her at his own stables, and they would stay at a coaching inn on the way to rest both themselves and the horses. She promised that she would return as soon as she could. She also insisted that she would ride cross saddle as the side saddle would be too uncomfortable for a long journey.

No one must know that I am travelling South.

She paid a deal of coin but at last everything was arranged to her satisfaction. She was a good judge of horseflesh and she had chosen a light part-thoroughbred mare who was sound and kind-of-eye but who Clara judged to be able to cover the ground at a good speed if necessary. The ostler agreed that the mare had both stamina and speed and was an excellent choice for such a journey.

It was early evening by the time she arrived back at her lodgings and she found that her maid had packed a valise full of a mass of garments she did not need. She explained patiently that she was not travelling by coach so she only needed a bag which could be slung over the pummel of a saddle and that she would need some victuals for her brother and herself as they wanted to travel with all speed and would only be stopping for one night at a coaching inn. When the household had retired, she found some of Jack's clothes and tried them on.

It is well that I am tall and that he is slender!

She did not sleep for the rest of the night but sat in a chair in her chamber, going over her plans and then, just before dawn, while it was still dark and before the household was about, she slipped outside and walked the short way to the stables.

Her horse was already saddled for her and if the yawning stable boy was surprised to see her dressed in male attire, he said nothing.

She thanked him and gave him a coin, then, as he held the mare's head for her, she swung herself up into the saddle, gathered the reins and trotted out of the yard. When she was out of sight of the yard, she stopped briefly to don Jack's hat, tucking her hair up underneath its brim.

Without close scrutiny, I should be able to pass for a young man.

The sun had only just risen when Clara crossed the Thames and headed South, leaving behind her the noise of trundling carts, shouts and curses, the sounds of London waking to a new day. Her spirits lifted.

It is so good to be on horseback again and to breathe fresh air. This may be a foolhardy venture but at least I am doing something.

As the morning wore on, the way became less populated and there were long stretches of empty road between towns and scattered villages and farms. The road was rough and stony in places and where she could she steered her horse onto the verges where the going was softer and the mare could stretch out at a canter. She noted the names of the places she passed through so that she could judge her progress and, although she saw coaches stopping at inns on occasion, she rode on past and only when the way was unpopulated did she rest herself and her horse, slipping from the saddle and letting the mare crop the grass and drink from a stream while she ate the food she had brought with her.

She had to pace her journey carefully for it was an endurance test for the mare. Clara did not gallop her even though, at first, the animal was eager, but wherever she could she kept her to a steady canter and walked her through the towns. The day wore on and the evening was closing in when at last she came into Hastings, by which time the horse was exhausted and Clara saddle sore. She enquired where to find a bed for the night and stabling for the horse and was directed to the Swan. She lowered her voice and kept her head bent when making the arrangements and hoped that the dark would help her disguise. Having reached her destination, she suddenly felt defeated. She was so tired that she could hardly put one foot in front of another and the enormity of the task of finding Will seemed overwhelming.

How will I ever find him if, indeed, he is still here?

She enquired at the Swan whether a Mr Will Fraser was staying there but the landlord shook his head and then excused himself.

'Forgive me sir,' he said, hardly glancing at her. 'But the night mail coach is due to leave and we are missing a passenger.' He rushed out of the door and Clara followed where there was now a good deal of hustle and bustle as the coach was being readied for departure.

'We can wait no longer,' shouted the driver and just then a large be-whiskered gentleman appeared, followed by a servant carrying his luggage. Clara watched as the servant pushed the latecomer's valise into the coach and the man, huffing and puffing, heaved himself after it.

The driver flicked his whip over the horses' backs and the coach lumbered out of the courtyard.

Where do I begin to look for Will? Must I enquire at every inn in the town?

Clara bit her lip and tried to work out her best course of action but she was so weary that she found logical thought impossible.

And as she stood there, irresolute, another figure came flying down the road, waving a letter in front of him.

'Am I too late,' he enquired breathlessly. 'Has the mail coach left?'

The landlord turned to him. 'Sorry sir, it's just gone.'

'No,' said the man, 'it is I who am at fault. I ran it too fine this time.'

Clara turned abruptly at the sound of his voice and she gasped as she looked at him as he stood beneath the lamp over the doorway. For a moment she thought it was Jack and her heart leapt with joy and, indeed, she was already running over to embrace him when she realised her mistake.

She stopped in her tracks.

'Will,'

Will swung round, his body tensing, and looked at what he thought was a young man at his side.

'Are we acquainted, sir?' he asked, and Clara could hear the caution in his voice.

'Will, it is Clara,' she whispered.

At first, he looked totally confused and then, as he peered at her, he saw the familiar features under the hat which was drawn down low over her brow.

'What are you doing here?' he whispered. 'For God's sake, Clara, you may have been followed.'

'Credit me with some intelligence,' she snapped. 'I have covered my tracks well and I'm here to pass on an urgent message.'

'From whom? I don't understand. What?'

He was still clutching the letter in his hand.

'We are attracting attention,' said Clara. 'Is there somewhere private where we can speak?'

'I cannot … I cannot stay any longer. I have an urgent appointment. I'm sorry Clara but it is of the utmost importance that I keep it.'

'Five minutes,' she said. 'Five minutes of your time is all I ask. I have ridden all the way from London to give you this intelligence, Will. You must listen to me.'

At last he seemed to focus on her. 'Then pray tell me quickly.'

So, as they walked a little way away from the entrance of the Swan, out of the hearing of others, Clara told him what she had found, how she had found it, and the name embedded in the love poem.

'I have certainly heard the name,' said Will. 'But I am not familiar with those in high office.'

'But I am, Will.' And she told him the man's role in Government.

'Good Lord, Clara. And you believe that this man is our traitor?'

She nodded. 'I think that Jack believed it.' She put her hand on his arm. 'Do not breathe a word of this to anyone. You are the only person I can trust with this intelligence. The only person that Jack would trust. And if you receive any instructions or messages purporting to come from the man, then you must ignore them. I know that is what Jack would say.'

'I should tell Montagu.'

'No. You must tell no one. Your brother left London trusting no-one except me and he could not even be sure that I would find his note or that I would understand what it meant. You must keep this knowledge to yourself until you find Jack.'

She looked at the letter in his hand. 'Is that dispatch for Montagu?'

He nodded.

'Then it is as well you missed the mail coach. Do not send it. I imagine that you are telling him that you are setting off for France?'

'Yes, now, immediately. But how did you know?'

'Deduction,' she said.

Will smiled. 'You were always a clever one.'

She frowned. 'Mail can be intercepted, Will. The world of spying is twisted and devious and there's no telling who else might see your dispatches. No doubt that is why Jack decided to act alone to find proof of his treachery. You must tell no-one the man's name.'

Will crumpled up the dispatch and put it in his pocket. 'Montagu already knows of my intention to travel to France,' he said. 'This dispatch merely gives him more details.'

'I'm sure Montagu is loyal,' said Clara, 'but Jack did not even tell him of his suspicions. The traitor is powerful, Will, and his reach is long. I imagine he will do anything to ensure he is not unmasked. We must pray that he or his colleagues are not already on your trail.'

Will put his hands on Clara's shoulders and turned her towards him.

'Bless you for trusting me with this knowledge and for coming all this way to do so. I swear I will not divulge it to anyone and I will do everything in my power to try and find Jack and protect him.'

'Be careful, Will.'

'And you – I hate to leave you here like this, unprotected in an unknown town. But I am already late for my rendezvous. Can you…?

'I can look after myself, Will. Now go quickly, and may God be with you.'

Chapter Fourteen

Will ran back to the Stag Inn, his thoughts in confusion. He had to believe that the resourceful Clara would make her way safely back to London without discovery but what if someone had been watching her lodgings and followed her?

She has risked so much to reach me. What if she is unmasked at the inn or set upon on her journey back to London? Will she be able to maintain her disguise? What if her horse is lamed on her journey home?

But then he forced himself to think more logically. Clara had laid a careful plan and made it known that she was travelling North, not South. Their home in Lincoln's Inn might be under surveillance but surely Clara's urgent journey to visit a sick parent would not be deemed suspicious? Will remembered Clara's childhood passion for tricks and puzzles and allowed himself a brief smile.

She and Jack are well matched. They are both clever and with a love of puzzles and the art of subterfuge. I should have foreseen that they would not share with me their secret love for one another.

He slowed to a walk for a moment to catch his breath.

But what am I to do with this knowledge passed on from Jack and why did he not tell his colleagues what he had discovered?

At the Stag, Armstrong and Tom the fisherman were waiting, Tom pacing up and down the street outside. Armstrong had Will's haversack packed and ready for him.

'What kept you?' asked Armstrong, handing it over.

'There was a delay at The Swan,' said Will.

'There's no time to waste,' said Tom. 'We must leave at once.'

Will nodded and shouldered his haversack. It was very dark now and the streets were deserted as they walked silently towards the cliffs, Tom holding a lantern to guide them. He was in an ill mood and swore at Armstrong when he stubbed his foot on a cobble and let out a cry of pain.

'Quiet man!'

No one spoke as they trudged forward and began climbing up the steep path, but Will knew that Armstrong was struggling to keep up and he was relieved when Tom reached a group of men working at something on the top of the cliff and stopped to exchange a few words with them. It was too dark to see exactly what was happening but it was obvious that something was being constructed – and beside the men there were two horse drawn carts.

Will and Armstrong hung back and waited for Tom to re-join them. Will was curious about what the men were doing and he was about to enquire when he remembered that he was supposed to have made this journey before so it was likely that he should know. He kept silent, but then Armstrong spoke for him.

'What were those fellows doing?' he asked as they continued walking.

'Setting up the derrick,' said Tom shortly.

'So they will be winching goods up from the shore then?'

'Aye,' said Tom.

'Ah,' continued Armstrong. 'Then they'll drive them to places of concealment, I warrant.'

Tom grunted and Will could sense his irritation but Armstrong kept questioning him.

'Where do they take the goods?' he asked.

Tom stopped suddenly and turned to Armstrong, holding the lantern to his face.

'Hold your tongue Sergeant,' he snapped. 'It's none of your bloody business.'

Armstrong said no more but just raised his eyebrows in the darkness.

They walked on in silence, then suddenly Tom stopped, looking out to sea. The other two followed his gaze and saw a light in the distance, flickering on and off. Neither Will nor Armstrong questioned Tom, but Armstrong whispered to Will.

'Do you reckon that's our vessel, sir?'

Will had no time to answer for suddenly Tom veered off to the right and then stopped. He waited for them to catch up and then he held the lantern up so they could see the deep fissure in the rock beneath them.

'This is our way in,' he said, and started easing himself down. As he reached the edge of the fissure, he extinguished his lamp and turned to the others. 'It is only a short drop into the cave.' And then, of a sudden, he had disappeared.

Gingerly, the others followed him. 'I hope you trust this man, sir,' whispered Armstrong as he eased himself over the edge. Will heard him land inside and utter a loud curse, then he, too, followed.

Tom had relit the lantern and Will and Armstrong marvelled at the sight before them. They were in a high natural tunnel with a sandy floor and walls which were cold and damp to the touch. Tom was already walking along the tunnel which sloped gently downwards for some way and then opened out into a larger cave in which were neatly stacked some barrels and boxes.

'So, not all the goods are winched up then,' muttered Armstrong.

Tom seemed to have recovered his humour. 'Some are stored here for later collection,' he said. 'Depends on their destination.'

'What do they contain?' asked Armstrong.

Tom shrugged. 'Brandy and gin,' he said. 'And French textiles. There's much demand for French textiles in London.'

Will thought back to the sumptuous furnishings he had seen at Montagu's house.

I wonder if some of those came from a less legitimate route than through those dealers he spoke of.

They walked on, the ground below them sloping ever downwards and before long they could hear the sound of waves breaking on the shore and then, of a sudden, they came out onto a small cove. Here there were more men sorting barrels and boxes at the entrance of the cave, some shouldering boxes or rolling barrels to be winched up to the cliff top, some taking them to be stored inside the cave.

Although Tom acknowledged the men with a nod, the group spoke only to direct others on where to place the goods and the only constant noises were the men's grunts of effort as they shifted them. Some glanced over at Will and Armstrong but most ignored them. Tom went to one of the men and they had a brief conversation in low tones, Tom nodding and gesturing, then he came back.

'The galley is anchored around the other side of the cove and most of the goods have been offloaded so we can row out to her now.' Then he led them down towards the water where several rowing boats were tied to jutting out pieces of rock. He gestured to one and told them to take off their boots, wade out to it and get on board.

As Will was helping Armstrong with his boots, he sensed the fear in the Sergeant's eyes. Although Will, too, was very uneasy, he tried to make light of their predicament.

'Never fear Sergeant,' he said. 'I'm a strong swimmer. If they tip us out, I'll hold you up.'

Armstrong didn't answer.

When they were seated, rocking fearfully in the shallows, Tom pushed them out into deeper water, jumped nimbly into the boat and took the oars. By now the moon was up but the sea below them was inky black and there was a swell which lurched the little vessel from side to side.

'We're in luck,' said Tom. 'No need for false light, nature's showing us the way.'

They could not see each other clearly but Will noticed that Armstrong was clinging to the side of the boat with his good arm and he could imagine the clenched jaw and terror writ large on his face.

The only sound was the splashing of the oars as they hit the water and, as they rowed further out, the slapping of the waves in the distance, reaching the shore. Tom was keeping the boat, as far as he was able, parallel to the shoreline and Will could sense the cliffs towering above them. And then they rounded the headland and there, ghostly in the moonlight, was the anchored galley, her sails down, gently rocking on the water ahead of them.

'I thought it would be a bigger vessel,' muttered Armstrong.

'Large enough for our purposes my friend,' said Tom.

As they came alongside, Will noticed the name painted in stark white letters on the vessel's stern.

Apus of London

He frowned. It seemed a fanciful name. He and Jack had studied the stars in their youth and Will knew Apus to be a small constellation in the Southern skies. He wondered how the galley had come by that name. Perhaps from sailors who had voyaged on merchant ships to the East Indies. Also, judging by the newness of the paint, the name had been recently changed; no doubt a common smuggler's trick.

His musings were cut short by a shout above them and a rope ladder was let down. He told Armstrong to climb up first so that he could stand below him and help him up if necessary, but Armstrong managed to struggle up the ladder on his own, breathing heavily and muttering oaths, then he was pulled up onto the deck by a couple of men. Will followed and they were immediately directed to sit close to the stern and keep quiet. They did as they were bid and heard around them the sound of more men coming up the ladder and some shifting and sliding of goods coming on board, accompanied by grunts and curses in low voices and the occasional gruff laugh.

When Will got to his feet to stretch his cramped legs the Master, a heavily bearded large man sporting a filthy jerkin and a cap rammed down on his head, immediately swore at him and told him to sit down.

Will apologised, but in that brief moment he had seen a barrel, not filled with liquor but with a false top into which gold ingots and guineas, some English newspapers and a heap of sealed letters were being stuffed with all haste.

The vessel was long and lay low in the water and Will noted that it could be propelled by oars as well as sails making it fast and easy to manoeuvre.

There was no need for light on board. The moon was full and the stars bright in a clear sky but the wind had dropped. The crew did not hoist the sails but as soon as the goods had been loaded and made fast, the anchor was pulled up and the men took the oars and began to row away from the coast and towards France. Will looked back towards Hastings where there were still a few points of light showing in houses in the town.

He could not know that there were other eyes watching their departure and another, faster, vessel, being readied for a voyage across the Channel.

Looking up at the night sky, Will mouthed a silent prayer to the God he had been brought up to believe in but now doubted, asking for His protection, and then he shuffled closer to Armstrong, who now had his back against the mast and legs stretched out in front of him, his face tense.

'I tell you, sir, I'd rather fight the French on land any day. I'm not suited to sea going.'

'I'm grateful for your company Sergeant.'

Armstrong grunted. He had already voided his stomach several times into the sea. 'How long must we endure this?' he whispered.

Will sighed. 'We shall be in France by tomorrow, Sergeant, you can be sure of that, but our speed will depend on the wind, whether it is for or against us. If we get a good breeze when they hoist the sails, then we shall make faster progress.'

They exchanged few words after that and eventually Armstrong lay down and drifted off into an uneasy, restless sleep, but Will stayed awake, watching the moon and the stars and pondering on the information that Clara had brought him. If Jack knew the identity of the traitor, why had he not exposed him? Was he still collecting evidence against him? Given the man's identity, would Jack be believed without hard evidence? All this swirled around in his head together with images of Clara, dressed in male clothes, her face strained as she revealed Jack's secret.

Only Clara would have the courage to lay a false trail, disguise herself as a man and ride those many miles to warn me.

Then his thoughts turned to the other news he had heard from Armstrong. That the Colonel of the Buffs, volunteers charged with fighting the smugglers, was none other than the father of his betrayer. The bile rose in his throat and he fought to suppress his anger and resentment.

I cannot fight old battles. I have a job to undertake, a brother to find and a spy to unmask.

At last he, too, lay down on the deck and closed his eyes, but his sleep was disturbed by vivid dreams and he was thankful when he was jerked awake by the crew pushing him out of the way so that they could hoist the sails. He stood up and stretched and looked across to the East where the dawn sky was streaked with red and orange and then, turning his head, he could just see, on the horizon, a glimpse of land.

The sails cracked as they filled with wind and during the next hour the galley made good speed towards the shore. They were within sight of land, and Will was already beginning to work out some sort of plan, when the Master suddenly gave a shout and let forth an oath. Will and Armstrong both looked up in surprise as the man pointed at a distant smudge.

'That'll be an English gunboat,' he said.

It was not long before he was proved right. The smudge soon formed into a vessel and it was heading in their direction at speed.

'Damnation!' muttered the Master, then he turned to Will. 'No point in trying to outrun it,' he said. 'It would only condemn us further. I don't want to know your business, sir, but I'd ask you to have a fine story ready for the Government men.'

Two of the crew immediately set to work to conceal anything which might condemn them. They opened the false top of the barrel and emptied it, concealing ingots in their shoes and coins in their pockets.

One of the men had a fistful of documents in his hand. Will was thinking fast.

'Give those to me,' he said. 'I'll put them in my haversack and concoct a likely story about them.'

The man looked at the Master who nodded. 'I hope, sir,' he said to Will, 'that you are a fine actor, otherwise we shall all be arrested.' Then he ordered the false barrel top to be smashed into small pieces and tossed overboard.

The Master ordered the crew to lower the sails and they waited as the gunboat grew ever closer.

Armstrong was by Will's side. 'Act the officer now, sir. Stand up straight, put your shoulders back and act affronted.'

'I'm not on the parade ground,' muttered Will, but unconsciously he did as the Sergeant said when the gunboat came alongside and two armed men leapt onto the galley's deck. The elder of the two introduced himself as the Lieutenant Commander of the gunboat and requested to search the galley. Will had, by now, transformed himself into an arrogant and well-bred officer of the sort he had never admired. He stood, legs braced and arms folded, and confronted the men. Then he proffered his hand to the Commander.

'Captain Fraser of the Highland Light Infantry, recently returned from Portugal,' he said. 'I would ask you not to impede our passage.'

'We have to search the vessel, sir,' said the Commander. 'Government orders.'

'Search all you wish,' said Will, hoping that any search would be cursory, 'but you will find nothing of interest.' He gestured towards the Master. 'I have employed this man and his crew to take me, in all secrecy, to rescue two escaped prisoners of war and to hand over certain secret documents to those who are working undercover for our Government.'

The Commander did not look convinced. 'This vessel looks mighty like a galley called the Queen Anne that's been seized before.'

'But as you can see,' said Will, his voice calm, although his heart was beating wildly in his chest, 'You are mistaken. This vessel is the Apus of London.'

He noted that the men exchanged glances and Will pressed his advantage.

'I'm sure you understand that there is information I cannot disclose to you, sirs. I am in the service of the British Government and I am acting under orders sent from London on the highest authority.' Then he took a couple of the sealed documents from his haversack and waved them under the men's noses. 'These contain the most confidential missives and must not, under any circumstances, fall into the wrong hands.'

'And what is your role, exactly, sir?'

Will raised an eyebrow and twisted his lips into what he hoped was a sarcastic smile.

'My dear Commander,' he said. 'Surely you know better than to ask.'

Both men were, by now, looking quite discomforted. Will continued. 'Now, we have done you the courtesy of stopping and allowing you on board. I beg that you return the favour and let us continue on our journey with all haste. There is a rendezvous I need to keep in France and the security of our country will be at considerable risk if I do not make contact with my agent at the appointed time.'

In the event, to Will's great relief, the men did not search the vessel but finally returned to the gunboat having shaken Will's hand and wished him God speed on his mission.

When the gunboat had left and the crew had, once more, hoisted the sails, Armstrong turned to Will.

'Lord, sir, Sally and Lottie would be proud of you. You've missed your calling. You should join them on the stage.'

Even the surly Master congratulated him on his performance and thanked him for his quick thinking. 'You gave a good impression of a military man, sir. I could almost believe you were an officer!'

Armstrong turned away to hide his smile but Will was sweating profusely and trembling with the strain of it.

How much more lying will I have to do on French soil? I am not suited to such deception.

Chapter Fifteen

Soon they were close enough to land to make out long stretches of sand backed by high dunes. The crew took down the sails and dropped anchor in the shallows.

'Is this the port?' asked Armstrong.

The Master gave a derisory laugh. 'No mistaking you for a sailor,' he said. 'No, the port of Gravelines is further North. It's well fortified and it's full of customs men though, in truth, they hardly care, but still, we don't take risks.' Then, casting a sideways glance at Will. 'Leastways not with spies. The coast's wild and unpopulated here and it suits our purpose – and yours, too, I warrant.'

It was the longest speech he had made and Will assumed that his acting skills with the gunboat Commander had softened the Master's attitude towards him and made him more voluble.

'And it's here that you exchange your … goods?' asked Armstrong.

'Aye,' said the Master. 'And one of your comrades will be here to meet you no doubt?'

'Yes,' said Will, remembering that Tom would have told the Master that Jack had been over to France only recently.

I dare not say too much in case I reveal my ignorance.

Will looked at Armstrong who immediately caught his drift.

'Our people keep a watch for your ship do they?' asked Armstrong.

The Master frowned. 'There's usually one of your comrades on lookout, yes.' He gestured to Will's haversack. 'They'll be waiting for those documents so you can save me a job and deliver them yourselves.'

Will did not dare to question the Master further in case he gave himself away.

But to whom should I deliver them, and where?

The Master stayed on the galley and Will and Armstrong waded ashore, following the crew members, holding their boots and haversacks clear of the water. When they reached the sands, Armstrong let out a huge sigh of relief.

'Lord, I am mighty pleased to be on dry land once more,' he said. Then, turning to Will. 'How's your French, sir? I warrant you'll be needing your language skills.'

'That is, indeed, a worry,' said Will as he pulled on his boots and helped Armstrong with his. 'Although we were both tutored in the language and I have a good understanding of it, Jack was the more fluent.'

'You spoke Spanish in the Peninsular, sir. And to my ears you sounded like a native.'

Will smiled. 'I won't deny that I have a good ear, and we were there long enough to become attuned, but my French speaking skills are rusty.'

'I thought every gentleman was taught to speak French.'

'It is the lingua franca, Sergeant, so it's useful to have the skill.'

The four crewmen climbed up and over the dunes and disappeared, leaving Will and Armstrong on the sands. Will looked around hopefully but there was no sign of anyone else.

'We must trust that our sailing friend speaks the truth and that someone will be here to meet us in due course,' he said.

'Umm. Perhaps they'll bring some food with them too. I've puked all my victuals into the sea and I'm fearsome hungry.'

'Be patient, Sergeant. We will have to tread very carefully now. Remember that Jack is not a military man. His contacts here will know him only as a Government agent and I shall, no doubt, have to pretend knowledge which I do not possess.'

'So, I'm not to call you Captain?'

'You should not in any circumstance, but certainly not now.'

'What shall I be then, sir. If you call me Sergeant, will that not cause suspicion?'

Will rubbed his chin. 'I could pass you off as my guard, perhaps?'

'What! A one-armed guard?'

'Can you think of a better pretence?'

They sat on the sands and watched the galley bobbing up and down in the shallows. They could see that the Master was moving about on board, adjusting ropes and no doubt making space for more goods. Before long, the crew and a few other men emerged from over the dunes. They had with them several barrels which they then lashed onto a crude raft which they floated in the shallows and pushed through the water to the galley where, with much heaving and cursing, they were loaded onto the deck. They went back for two more loads before their French companions vanished back over the dunes.

One of the crew members came over to Will. 'I saw your contact up there,' he said, jerking his thumb behind him. 'He says he'll wait for you in the usual place.'

'And where do you reckon that is?' whispered Armstrong when the man had left.

Will frowned. 'I cannot guess, but I would hope the contact will tire of waiting and come and find us.'

'Will this deception work, sir? Will they not be suspicious of an agent who is ignorant of the arrangement?'

'Possibly, but I am relying that they will think that I am my brother.'

Will did not confide his own worries to the Sergeant.

This deception is fraught with danger. I can so easily give myself away.

As soon as the goods were on board, the anchor was pulled up and the Master raised a hand in farewell. Then the galley was on her way, much lower in the water, now, weighed down by her heavy cargo. Will and Armstrong watched as the sails were hoisted again and the craft moved away from the shore.

Then they waited, Armstrong growing tetchier by the minute and complaining of hunger, Will fearful of what was to come and how he might convince some unknown contact that he was Jack.

Neither of them had noticed that, while the loading and unloading was going on, another boat had sailed quietly into the next cove and put down its anchor, nor that someone had disembarked from the boat and, using the dunes as cover, was gradually coming closer to them, keeping his head down and moving slowly and stealthily, occasionally dropping down on all fours to avoid being seen. Now he was concealed in a sandy hollow not far behind them, watching and waiting.

***

The tide had turned and was steadily creeping up the beach. Will got stiffly to his feet.

'We shall have to retreat, Sergeant. The water is coming in fast.'

They clambered up into the dunes. They were high and difficult for Armstrong to climb but he clung on to the spiky grass which grew where it could on their sandy surface and finally joined Will at the top of a high one which afforded them a view of the surrounding landscape. Will shaded his eyes and looked around the coastal land beyond which was wild and seemingly unpopulated.

'Well Sergeant,' he said, 'You are a resourceful fellow. Have you any idea what we should do now?'

'Find something to eat,' muttered Armstrong, then he cleared his throat. 'I reckon we should start walking inland, sir. Your man's not coming down to the sea, it seems.'

Will shouldered his haversack and smiled at Armstrong. 'Any idea in which direction Sergeant?'

Armstrong uttered an oath and started to march forward but the dunes stretched ahead and the ground was very uneven. Sand kept getting into his boots and he made slow progress. They had covered very little distance when a figure rose suddenly from behind a dune in front of them. Will immediately put his hand on his sword, but when the man spoke to him in English, he removed it.

'Christ, Jack. What in God's name are you doing here? This is idiocy. Why are you showing yourself like this? Why are you not with Marie?' Then, when Will was trying to think of a suitable response, the man continued. 'I thought they had sent a new recruit who was unaware of the meeting place.' Then he frowned. 'Is it you, then, who has the letters for me? Don't tell me you have been back to London? And who is this?' he said, gesturing at Armstrong.

'A trusted companion,' said Will.

The man frowned. 'If you say so.' He stared at Armstrong who braced his shoulders to make himself look suitably trustworthy, then turned back to Will.

'If it were anyone else who came with an unknown companion…' Then he put a hand out to shake Armstrong's, withdrawing it hastily as he realised his mistake. 'Jean Beasant, at your service.'

'Sergeant Armstrong,' replied Armstrong.

Beasant frowned. 'A military man?'

'Indeed,' said Will quickly. 'He has helped me in ways you cannot imagine and I trust him with my life.'

'Just as well,' said Jean, drily. '

Will dug in his haversack. 'I have the letters for you,' he said, handing them over.

Jean took them. 'They will probably contain nothing but false information,' he said. Our traitor, whoever he is, has been mighty industrious, the bastard. I suppose there is no more intelligence on who he might be?'

It was on the tip of Will's tongue to say the name when he remembered Clara's words. 'Trust no-one.' He shook his head.

'But you have your suspicions?'

'Suspicions, yes,' said Will carefully. 'But with no proof …'

'And you cannot reveal …?'

'I dare not, Jean. If I am right then the repercussions will be dire and if I am wrong, I will have falsely accused an influential man and I myself will be punished. As you know, I was in fear of my life when I fled London.'

'And yet you have been back? I did not realise. I had no word from Marie that you were no longer with her.'

Who is Marie? Has she been hiding Jack? Jack must trust her – and Jean, too.

'I went back briefly to try and gather more information.'

'But you were not successful?'

'Alas, no. And the place was too hot for me. I was attacked by some villains when I was there and I don't doubt that they were hired to kill me. I am sure that the traitor is on my trail and wants me dead, which is why I have removed myself from London and come back here.'

Jean nodded. 'Marie is discreet and your hiding place in her barn is ideal. You will be safer here while you try to find a way of interpreting that letter and you'll be more likely to do that on this side of the Channel. If the letter proves the man's treachery, then we can trap the bastard. But for God's sake, Jack, be careful.'

Will nodded but his thoughts were racing.

What letter?

Armstrong had said nothing during this exchange but now he addressed Jean.

'I am here to protect him,' he said.

Will put an arm on Armstrong's shoulder. 'Even without one of his arms he is a prodigious fighter and swift to see danger. Whereas I …'

Jean smiled. 'You, Jack, are a scholar, a diplomat and a patriot. But no one would call you a fighting man.'

Armstrong started to smile and then quickly composed his features. 'Will you take us to this Marie's place?' he asked. 'We are both mighty hungry and no doubt she'll have something to feed us.'

Jean frowned and turned to Armstrong. 'Jack knows the way, you have no need of an escort. Marie lives yonder, at a small farm to the North.'

Will thought fast. 'Of course,' he said. 'But if you have the time, Jean, I would very much value your ideas on who else I can approach to unlock the secrets of that letter. Your knowledge of the network here is a deal better than mine. We can talk on the way, can we not.' Will looked about him. 'This place makes me uneasy. We are very exposed and, as you say, it is better that I am not seen in public.'

Jean shrugged and patted his pockets which now contained the documents which Will had brought him. 'I need to go through these with all haste,' he said. 'But I'll walk with you until our paths separate.'

They set off and, as they left the dunes behind them, they made better progress over the flat heathland.

***

None of them had noticed the other man lying still as a stone in his sandy hiding place, curled up in a hollow beneath a dune, his face hidden by a hood. He had overhead their exchange, including the mention of Marie's farm and the barn. As soon as Will, Armstrong and Jean were out of sight, he headed North, hugging the coastline and when he finally spotted the farm buildings in the distance, with a wood behind them, he made a detour, coming into the woods from behind.

Chapter Sixteen

Jack Fraser sat on a stool inside one of the empty stalls inside the big stone barn. Marie had given him the stool and a small table and, at first, he had kept them in the cavity beneath the floor of the barn where he had been sleeping on a rough straw pallet. But it was pitch dark in that under-croft and the light of a candle had not been strong enough for his purposes. He knew that he must remain concealed but he needed more light and he reckoned that he would be at little risk. No stranger had been near the place since he had been hiding here. He had been visited by Jean once and every day Marie brought him food, but otherwise the only sounds came from the crying of the seagulls or the occasional barking of the farm dog.

There was plenty of light here, in the main body of the barn. It streamed through the missing top of the old half door and from the open space beneath the apex of the roof timbers so he had brought the stool and table up so that he could do his experiments with more ease.

In his hands he held a sheet of paper, already soiled, crumpled and slightly burnt at its edges and this held the secret he needed to unlock. He had intercepted it on its journey from a high-ranking Government official together with others from the same source. The other letters were routine and he delayed them no longer but sent them on their way but this one's addressee had intrigued him and when he had opened it he realised at once that it had been written in invisible ink, for it was blank.

At first he had applied all the standard ways of bringing the writing out of the blank sheet of paper – applying heat to it and treating it to various chemicals, all to no avail. And it was then that he realised that the man who had sent it must have had access to a more advanced process – a process to which The Alien Office was not privy. He also knew that the French had made great progress in this area. It was more than likely, therefore, that both the sender and the recipient of the letter had access to a new, French process. Which was why he had absented himself from London so quickly. He knew that it would immediately be suspected that he had taken the letter and he also knew that his only chance of unlocking its secrets would be by painstaking experimentation. When he reached France he had asked Jean Beasant to enquire from his fellow agents if they had any intelligence of new chemicals used by the French but Jean had drawn a blank.

As he set about starting again to try and unravel the letter's secret, his thoughts went back to the message he had left in the desk in his room at Mrs Baxter's lodging house.

If I am killed will anyone else uncover the traitor? Will my Clara find my clumsy coded poem? And if she does, to whom will she show it? And what if I am wrong? What if I have accused a man falsely?

Jack had some knowledge of chemistry and reactions of certain chemicals upon one another and Marie had acquired for him a range of different ones. There was a row of small bottles lined up on the table in front of him and all morning he had been, yet again, mixing, applying, heating and cooling. Now, at last, the latest mixture he had applied was bringing the words from the paper and he sat, reading and re-reading what it revealed.

This was not what I was expecting.

***

The man was at the edge of the woods, now, hidden from sight. In the distance he could see Will, Armstrong and Jean walking towards the farm. Then he saw them pause where their paths divided.

He wasted no more time but crept out from the woods. He was so quiet that even the old farm dog did not hear him as he edged round the barn.

At the half door he peered inside, his eyes adjusting to the muted light within. He saw Jack sitting on the stool, holding up the paper and, even from where he was standing, he could see that it was covered in writing. He swore under his breath and reached for his pistol. Then he opened the bottom of the half door and went inside.

Jack had been so lost in thought that it took him a moment to realise that he was not alone then he jumped when he suddenly caught sight of the man.

Immediately, he leapt to his feet still holding the letter.

'I'll take that Jack,' said the man.

Jack stared at him. At first he'd not recognised him, dressed in the black cloak and with the cowl over his face but the moment he spoke, he knew who it was.

'Blackmail,' said Jack, his voice hoarse. 'You were blackmailed.'

The man nodded and raised his pistol.

***

As they walked together, Will questioned Jean Beasant, but in very general terms, about the French network of Royalists who wanted Napoleon Bonaparte toppled from power. He was aware, all the time, that Jack would already have most of this knowledge so he tried not to entangle himself and Armstrong, sensing his predicament, intervened with ingenuous questions from time to time, earning him exasperated looks from Jean.

They saw no one on their walk. Once or twice Jean stopped and looked about him then, satisfied that they were not being observed, walked on. At length, their track forked and Jean bade them farewell.

'I'll visit you soon, Jack,' he said. 'And be careful, I beg you.'

'Where's this Marie live then?' asked Armstrong.

Jean frowned, his irritation with Armstrong evident. He pointed. 'The cottage over there, by the farm buildings.' Then he continued. 'I am very surprised that she did not let me know that you had left, Jack.'

'It was a sudden decision,' said Will.

Armstrong had shaded his eyes and was staring at the small group of farm buildings some distance ahead of them.

'It's a mighty small cottage,' he murmured. 'Where did she conceal the … Mr Fraser.'

Jean muttered something in French and looked at Will, his eyebrows raised. Will shrugged and smiled back, hoping this was a suitable response.

'Of course she did not have him in the house, man. As I said, he was in the barn nearby where there is a false floor. Now, enough of all your questions. I must bid you both good-day.'

Once Jean was out of hearing Will put an arm round Armstrong's shoulders. 'Thank the Lord for your quick thinking, Sergeant. Our friend Monsieur Beasant may think you are a blundering idiot asking all those questions, but you played the part well.'

'Happy to oblige, sir,' said Armstrong, grinning.

They continued to walk on towards the farm buildings.

'I have to admit that I am mighty nervous, Sergeant.'

'Is this the end of our journey?'

'I sincerely hope it is and that we shall find my brother at last.'

'And if we do, what then?'

'What then indeed?'

Neither of them spoke as they came nearer. The place seemed unkempt and deserted though there were chickens wandering about, pecking on the ground, and a dog barked at their approach but it was either inside the cottage or tied up for it didn't come to greet them.

'Should we knock on the door, sir?'

'No, I think we should go straight to the barn.'

They kept looking from side to side but the place was eerily quiet and when Will trod on a twig, the sound of its snapping was unnaturally loud in the silence.

And then, suddenly, there was the sound of a gunshot and almost immediately afterwards someone burst out from the barn door. Dressed in black and with his hair awry and the cowl which had been covering his face thrown back, he was sprinting towards the woods at the back of the farm.

For a moment, Will stopped in his tracks as the shocking sound of the gunshot broke the silence, but only for a moment and then, with sudden clarity, he realised who the man was and with a sick understanding knew what he had just done and how he, Will, had enabled him to do it.

He dropped the haversack he was carrying and yelled at Armstrong to go inside the barn and then he turned and ran towards the woods, unsheathing his sword as he did so. Fury and shame were pumping through his body but he tried to think clearly as he ran.

He has a gun. He will kill me if he can. I should use my pistol

But then he realised he had left it in his haversack.

I'll lose sight of him if I go back.

He ran on, crashing through the farmyard, scattering the chickens which clucked and flapped in fear, and on into the woods. The man was well ahead of him now and he could hear his heavy footsteps and the sound of undergrowth snapping beneath them.

He must have someone waiting for him on the coast. If he can get back to a boat, he'll escape me.

Will redoubled his efforts, forcing himself to run faster, leaping over obstacles in his way. Then he stopped for a moment to listen and realised that the sounds ahead of him had ceased. He looked this way and that but could see no sign of the man. Very cautiously, Will made his way forward, but still there was no sound in the woods save some birdsong.

And then it came, another gunshot, sending the birds flapping and squawking out of the trees. It missed Will's head by inches but it enabled him to gauge its direction and he had a glimpse of a black cloak concealed behind the broad trunk of a tree.

Any moment and he will fire again. He may not realise I have spotted him.

Will ran straight for the tree, so filled with fury that it hardly mattered to him that he was in mortal danger. When he reached it, the man was in the process of raising his arm to fire again but Will was quicker. He knocked the pistol from his hand with his sword and then pushed him to the ground.

And then he was on him. The man screamed for mercy but Will was deaf to his pleas, and plunged his sword into the man's heart.

He watched as the life drained from James Montagu, the man's eyes staring up at him, the body twitching and blood coming out of his mouth and staining the earth red.

Will did not know how long he stood there looking down at it, tears flowing freely down his face, but at length he became aware of Armstrong's presence beside him and turned towards him.

'Sergeant,' he whispered.

Armstrong nodded. 'Bastard,' he said, his voice gruff.

'Is Jack dead?'

'Aye. Shot through the heart.'

Will flung his sword to the ground and dropped to his knees. 'And I am the cause,' he said. 'It is my fault. I have blundered into this and ruined everything, Sergeant. Sweet Christ how can I live with myself?'

There was still nobody about and the only sound, now, came from the calling of the seagulls as they wheeled and drifted on the breeze coming in from the sea. Armstrong cleared his throat. 'Come on, sir,' he said. 'Do not torture yourself. You cannot have known.' He put out his good hand to haul Will to his feet then he looked down at the body.

'Why?' he asked.

'What?'

'Why did he do it?'

But Will had no answer and said nothing. Armstrong frowned.

'Think sir. What did your brother have? It must have been mighty important for Montagu to kill for it.'

Still Will said nothing and continued to look down at the body, shaking his head.

'What did that Jean fellow say? Was there something about a letter? If we can find the letter, maybe we can salvage something from all this.'

Will stared at Armstrong. 'Nothing can be salvaged,' he said flatly. 'My brother is dead and I am guilty.'

'You are consumed with grief, sir, but let us think what your brother would want you to do. We can at least search the man's body.'

Will had started to shake. Armstrong glanced at him and sighed, then he knelt down beside the body and began to search it, clumsily pulling up Montagu's shirt, never flinching at the sight of the deep wound beneath. Finding nothing there, he delved into the pockets of the dark cloak and drew out a crumpled sheet of paper. He handed it to Will who looked at it without comprehension.

'I … I can make no sense.'

Armstrong got to his feet and took the paper from Will's shaking hands. Haltingly, for his reading skills were not good, he read it. Then he looked up.

'It seems to me,' he said quietly, 'that this is all the proof you need, sir. This letter will bring that highly placed traitor to justice, I fancy.'

At last, Will focussed on the letter, taking it from Armstrong. It was written in a bold and confident hand with a legible signature at the bottom. The signature of the man suspected by Jack. The name he had left in code for Clara to find.

The letter was burnt at the edges and stained but the writing was legible.

"Destroy this immediately you have read it, James, but I wish to make clear that henceforth you will work with me to suppress any Royalist revolution in the Republic and you will pass on to me all intelligence sent to you by British agents in France. You know the penalties if you do not. I have proof of your liaison with H and will expose you as a sodomite."

Armstrong looked at Will. 'A compelling reason for the man to change sides, I warrant.' Then, when Will said nothing, he continued. 'It's the death penalty, aint it, for sodomites?'

Will nodded remembering, suddenly, that first visit to Montagu's house when he was so discomforted by their unexpected presence and the whiff of that expensive cigar smoke which hung in the air.

He looked down at Montagu's body. 'Perhaps by killing him I have spared him a more gruesome death,' he said quietly.

Armstrong put his hand on Will's shoulder. 'Between you, you and your brother have uncovered a traitor. Someone so close to Government that he would not be suspected without proof. You have done your country a service, sir.'

'I led Montagu to Jack.'

Armstrong had no answer to that.

They said nothing as they walked slowly back to the barn. Still there was no sound from the cottage and the chickens continued to peck at the ground and the dog set up its barking again.

Inside the barn, Will knelt by Jack's body and stroked his hair. 'If only we had been quicker to reach you Jack. If only you had been able to get back to London and present this proof.'

'But now you will do it for him,' said Armstrong firmly.

'I do not know how …'

'We shall find a way, sir.' He cleared his throat. 'What would you like to do … with his body? And with Montagu's? We cannot leave them here.

Will shook his head. 'I'd like Jack to have a decent burial.'

'We shall have to hurry then, sir. There's no knowing when this Marie will be back.'

Between them they carried Jack's body into the woods behind the farm and, using a spade he found in a shed, Will dug two graves in the soft earth under a hornbeam tree. When he had finished, he and Armstrong tidied up the surface as best they could and Will bowed his head and put his hands together. He commended the souls of the dead men to God, his voice cracking at the mention of Jack's name.

'Huh!' said Armstrong. 'It was mighty generous of you to say a prayer for that bastard Montagu.'

'Do not blame him too harshly Sergeant. His position was impossible.'

Armstrong raised his eyes to the sky but said nothing.

When they came out of the woods, Armstrong stopped suddenly.

'There's someone about,' he said, pointing ahead to a woman in the farmyard throwing grain to the chickens squawking and flapping around her. A pony and cart stood outside the cottage door.

Will hardly registered.

'Sir,' said Armstrong, shaking Will's arm. 'Should we go and speak with her?'

'I do not know, Sergeant. What does it matter now?'

But the decision was made for them for in that moment, the woman looked up from her task and noticed them emerging from the trees. She did not seem startled but scattered the last of the grain and then started to walk towards them, chattering away in

French and gesturing, pointing at Armstrong and obviously expecting an answer.

'What's she saying, sir?'

The woman spoke with a heavy local accent and Will was trying to make sense of it. He put up his hand to stop her and explained who he was, told her that Jack had been killed and asked her to go and fetch Jean Beasant.

The woman stared at him, understanding gradually dawning, and started to back away, but Will persevered, calling her Marie this time, assuring her again that he was a friend, that he had tried to prevent Jack's death and asking again that she fetch Jean as a matter of urgency.

At last, Marie seemed to understand, though it was obvious that she was very frightened. Armstrong made some gestures indicating that they were hungry and she took them into her kitchen. It was apparent that she had just returned from market for the table was covered with supplies. She pointed to some bread and cheese and then ran out of the cottage, scrambled up onto her cart and urged the pony in the shafts into a smart trot.

Armstrong fell upon the food but Will simply stood and stared out of the window.

'Come sir, you must eat.'

But Will shook his head.

'What did you say to her?' asked Armstrong, between mouthfuls.

'I asked her to fetch Jean Beasant,' said Will.

'And do you reckon she'll do your bidding?'

Will shrugged. 'I hardly care,' he said. 'I am a condemned man, a murderer. My life is forfeit whatever happens.'

'That's no talk for a soldier.'

'I am not a soldier. I am nothing.'

Chapter Seventeen

Marie did not let them down. Jean Beasant returned to the cottage with her and as Will seemed too stunned to speak, Armstrong did his best to answer the questions that came thick and fast. Jean expressed at first disbelief and then fury at Montagu's treachery and genuine sorrow at Jack's death. Marie sat with them staring at Will, tears never far away, and Will was silent until Armstrong finally nudged him.

'For God's sake, sir,' he said quietly. 'Explain to them. For your brother's sake! I cannot tell them the whole story.'

'My life is ended Sergeant. What does it matter now?'

Jean stood up suddenly, scraping his chair back on the stone floor. He went over to Will and shook his shoulders. 'For the love of Christ, man, pull yourself together. We have a whole network of good people putting their lives at stake every day to try and undermine Napoleon's republic. Your sorrow is great but we have all lost loved ones in this struggle. Now, your Sergeant tells me you have proof which will condemn the traitor.'

Suddenly Will seemed to come back from the dark place in which his thoughts were trapped. He sighed. 'You are right, Jean. Jack had obtained proof – though God knows how – and it was this proof that Montagu sought, and found.' He drew out the letter from his pocket and handed it over.

Jean took it and then looked up. 'By the blood of Christ,' he murmured. 'So our traitor is hiding in plain sight in the British Government?'

Will nodded.

'And does Reeves know?'

'Who?'

'John Reeves. Head of the Alien Office.'

'No. Had he known, then presumably he would have taken action.'

'Then he must be informed at once. It is your duty to take this to him immediately.'

Armstrong was watching Will closely. It was as if the word duty had struck a distant chord, of recent times when his duty as an officer was not in question. He looked up then and his voice was firmer.

'Then I will need your help to get back across the Channel,' he said.

***

So it was that, just three days later, Will and Armstrong found themselves back in London. The first part of the journey had not been pleasant, in a fishing boat and in lashing rain, but Armstrong, though sick as a dog, had not complained. And this time they had landed in Dover and caught the coach from there to the capital.

Though he was heartsick and exhausted, Will knew where his first duty lay and it was not with Reeves. He headed for Lincoln's Inn despite Armstrong urging him to go straight to the Alien Office.

The moment he walked into Clara's apartment and she saw his face, she knew. She came up to him immediately and took both his hands in his.

'What's happened, Will? Did you find him?'

And then, standing there, looking her in the eye, Will recounted the whole sorry saga. He left nothing out.

Gradually, as understanding dawned, she withdrew her hands.

'So, you led Montagu to Jack?'

He nodded. 'I shall never forgive myself.'

She said nothing but walked over to the window and looked out onto the courtyard below. It was still raining.

'I'm so sorry,' said Will, acutely aware of the inadequacy of the remark. Clara said nothing.

'What will you do?' he asked.

Her reply was cold. 'I shall go North to my parents and tell them that Jack is dead. And you should do the same. You should go to your family and break the news to them in person.'

'Then we will travel together,' said Will.

'I think not.'

She called for her maid. 'Be so good as to show Mr Fraser out,' she said. Then went back to the window and did not turn round again when her maid came in and Will took his leave.

***

At the Alien Office, Will announced himself as Jack Fraser, sick at the deception but reckoning that he would be immediately ushered into the presence of John Reeves. He was right and he soon found himself confronting the head of the Alien Office across that same desk where Montagu had so recently outlined his plans.

Reeves was smiling and shook his hand enthusiastically.

'My God, Jack, it is good to see you.' He gestured at Will's attire. 'I see from the state of you that you have come immediately from the coast. Let me offer you a little refreshment and then we have much to discuss.'

Will cleared his throat. 'Sir, I am not Jack, I am his brother Will.'

Reeves hesitated in the process of unstopping a cut glass decanter of fortified wine which stood on a table against the wall. He peered at Will.

'If that is so, then the likeness is quite remarkable.' He frowned and replaced the stopper carefully in the top of the decanter, his initial warmth replaced by an expression of wariness.

'I have to tell you Mr Fraser, that I am not happy that you deceived me in this way, that you used guile to gain access to my office. I hope that your deception means that you have news for me, that you have found your brother?'

'We found him, sir, yes,' said Will slowly. 'But … but I also led his murderer to him.'

'What!'

Will nodded. 'It is something for which I shall never forgive myself but I very much regret to inform you that when we found Jack, he was dead, shot through the heart.'

Reeves continued to stare at him in disbelief.

'I buried him myself, sir,' said Will. 'Under a hornbeam tree in a wood not far from Gravelines.'

There was a long silence, then Reeves shook his head and said quietly.

'Jack was one of my very best agents. What a loss to this office, and to the country.' There was another silence and then he continued. 'Do you know the identity of the man who killed him?'

Will took the burnt paper from the pocket of his coat and handed it to Reeves.

'This is the proof of the identity of your traitor, sir,' he said. 'And from this I imagine that you will be able to deduce who it was that killed Jack.'

Reeves took the paper and smoothed it out on the top of his desk. He let out an oath as he read it. Finally he looked up.

'Are you telling me that Montagu killed your brother because he was being blackmailed?'

'It would seem so, sir. We found this letter on his person.'

'And where is Montagu now?'

Will looked down at the magnificent woven Turkey rug beneath his feet. 'I caught him fleeing from the murder scene, sir,' he said quietly. Then he drew himself up and looked Reeves in the eyes. 'I killed him, sir, and although I expect no mercy, I should say that I was blinded by fury and misery that I had inadvertently caused my brother's death.'

Reeves regarded Will for a long time and Will did not flinch. Then Reeves looked again at the paper in his hands. He tapped the signature with his finger.

'You know who this is, Fraser?'

Will nodded. 'His signature is clear. An influential man in the Government.'

Reeves began to pace up and down. 'Indeed. He has risen to prominence since fleeing France at the time of the Revolution. He is an aristocrat and would undoubtedly have been guillotined in those violent times had he not escaped. He railed against Bonaparte and the Republicans and was trusted by our royalist contacts in France, but it seems now that he was a double agent. Instead of trying to undermine the Republic and support uprisings against Napoleon, he has been passing on information about our plans to the agents of our enemies.'

Reeves stopped his pacing and came to a halt beside Will. 'I am very grateful for this piece of paper, Fraser. It explains the inexplicable.'

'What will happen to him?'

Reeves sighed. 'It happens that I asked to go and call on him yesterday but a message came back that he was away for a few days.'

'Do you think he has heard …?'

'Oh yes, he will have heard. He has eyes and ears everywhere. I would place money on his being back in France now and under the protection of the regime where he is being congratulated on how he has ruined our plans for …'

Then suddenly he seemed to remember that Will was not his brother.

'Forgive me. Your resemblance is so marked, I find myself thinking you are Jack.'

And then, finally, Reeves went back to the decanter. This time he unstopped it and poured a generous measure into two glasses. He handed one to Will and gestured for him to sit down. Reeves drew up a chair opposite him.

'I'm told you fought bravely in the Peninsular, Fraser.'

'No more than many others,' said Will.

'But then you left in disgrace?'

Will took a gulp of his drink and then wearily rubbed his brow.

'You are well informed, sir.'

Reeves indulged in one of his long silences and Will shifted in his chair.

'Some say you were harshly judged,' he said at last.

'From whom did you hear that, sir?'

'From James Montagu.'

'Perhaps he, too, was harshly judged,' said Will quietly.

'Indeed. Secrets about one's tastes in … one's proclivities, once unmasked, are ripe for exploitation. He was a brilliant man, Fraser, and he served me well in the past. It is very unfortunate that he gave in to blackmail.'

'Would our traitor have exposed him?'

Reeves shrugged. 'Possibly. Though I imagine the threat was enough.'

Will nodded, finished his drink and stood up. 'Thank you for seeing me, sir.'

Reeves did not move but gazed down into his glass. 'What will you do now, Fraser?'

Will sighed. 'I'll have little choice, sir. I'm not only a disgraced soldier but a murderer and have caused the murder of my beloved brother. I imagine that the full force of the law will come down on me for Montagu's death.'

Reeves continued to stare into his glass. 'You killed men on the battlefield, did you not?'

'Of course. But that was war.'

Reeves got to his feet. 'And so is this, Fraser. Although this was an act carried out in vengeance for your brother's death, you killed a man who was helping our enemies. Montagu may have been blackmailed but he was betraying his country. He killed your brother because he was the only person who had proof of our traitor's identity. I imagine he found that proof on your brother's person, and no doubt, had he had time, he would have destroyed it. As it was, he heard you coming, put it in his pocket to destroy later, and fled.'

'Or perhaps he was going to show it to you?'

'Hmm. You are generous to think so, Fraser, but I doubt it. Remember, he had betrayed us and he would have faced the gallows if he had been branded a sodomite.'

Another long silence.

'One thing I cannot understand,' said Will. 'Is why Jack did not come to you sooner.'

Reeves shrugged. 'He knew I would have needed proof to accuse such a powerful figure. I suspect Jack needed time to expose the letter.'

Will frowned. 'What do you mean?'

Reeves picked up the paper and took it over to the window.

'The French have perfected the art of invisible writing,' he said. 'There are various ways of exposing it but we do not know all of them. Jack intercepted the letter addressed to Montagu. His suspicions must have been aroused when he saw that the paper was blank and he would have guessed that it contained a secret message. We know he did not alert Montagu – and we cannot know why not, but being Jack, his reasons would have been sound.

When he failed to uncover the message here he must have taken the decision to travel to France where our agents have more knowledge of the necessary chemicals needed to reveal its contents.' Reeves sighed. 'I think he may have known that Montagu could be a target for blackmail.'

'And Montagu knew it had been intercepted by Jack?'

Reeves shrugged. 'He must have guessed when Jack disappeared so suddenly. He was a brilliant man and extremely well informed.'

'It is a sorry mess, sir, and I am ashamed of my part in it.'

Reeves clapped him on the shoulder. 'I am deeply saddened by Jack's death,' he said, but you have done us a great service. We know now who our traitor is, we know that he had details of our planned operation and that he caused it to be aborted.'

'And Jack was part of that operation?'

Reeves nodded. 'He and Montagu were masterminding it and many of our most trusted agents were involved,' he said. Then he sighed. 'Since it will not now happen, I suppose I can tell you a little about it.' He drained the last dregs from his glass. 'Our traitor knew the identity of many of our royalist agents and their activities and was aware that they were plotting a huge insurrection in Northern France. We had been working towards this for months and everything was in place.'

'And he will have told his masters?'

Reeves nodded. 'Now the French spymasters will have all this information together with the identities of the agents involved.' He paused, then cleared his throat. 'And Napoleon's Minister of Police, Joseph Fouché, is known for his brutality. He will, without doubt, seek revenge.'

'Good God, sir, that is a sorry blow.'

'Indeed. And it means that we have much to do to rebuild our network, to recruit new and unsuspected agents.'

Will was aware that the day was advancing and that he was due to travel North on the coach.

'Sir, I have to go North to inform my family of Jack's death,' he said. 'I have booked a space on a coach which leaves shortly. I must take my leave.' He picked up his hat and headed for the door.

Reeves put up his hand. 'Just a moment, Will,' he said.

He calls me by my Christian name. I am surprised at such intimacy.

'Sir?'

'Jack is someone who I trusted utterly and it seems to me that you are cut from the same cloth.'

Will frowned.

'I wonder,' said Reeves, 'if you would consider becoming one of this new network?'

Will turned back.

What have I got to lose? No one else will employ me. And he will save me from prison – or worse.

'It will be a way of serving my country, sir. I would be honoured to join you.' Then as Reeves came over to him to shake his hand, he added. 'On one condition.'

'Which is?'

'That Sergeant Armstrong is also recruited.'

Reeves said nothing.

'He was with me in Portugal, sir. I trust him in the same manner in which you trusted Jack. We have been through much together. He may have been injured in the war but he has the heart of a lion – and he has proved that he can keep his mouth shut.'

Another long silence and then 'Very well, Will.'

Chapter Eighteen

Sergeant Armstrong had never been to the theatre before but his reluctance to enter the Theatre Royal in Drury Lane was overcome by Sally's agreement to meet him for a late supper after the show.

'It's not all toffs that come to see it,' she'd said. 'All the quality are in their private boxes and in the seats round the edge but there's cheap tickets for the benches in the pit.'

So he'd joined the mass of folk streaming in through the doors of the theatre. Most of them were finely dressed in their silks and feathers and he noticed some gentlemen in uniform amongst them, but there were a goodly number of ordinary folk like him, too, heading for the benches in the pit and there was much good natured shoving and banter as they found themselves somewhere to sit.

'Back from the wars?' asked the man next to Armstrong, gesturing at the Sergeant's empty sleeve.

'Aye.'

A rowdy party pushed past them, bumping into Armstrong and almost unseating him.

'Have a care,' said his companion. 'That's a wounded soldier there!'

The party turned and apologised as they sat down on the bench, squeezing in where they could.

Armstrong stared around him, observing the folk in the tiers above, the women chattering behind their fans to their finely dressed escorts. There was intricately patterned plasterwork between each tier and the royal coat of arms above the stage itself. The whole theatre was lit up by the candlelight coming from the many chandeliers hung from the ceiling and at intervals on every level. He noticed there were private boxes, too, right on the stage itself. Most were full of grand ladies and gentlemen but two, the grandest of all, with red silk on their fronts, one on each side of the stage, were empty. Despite the crowds and the jostling for space, he saw no one enter them. He turned to his companion pointing to them.

'Why are there no folk in those?'

'Ah, those are the royal boxes. One for the King and one for the Prince.'

Armstrong frowned.

'They don't get along, the King and the Prince,' said his companion, 'so when they both come to see a performance, one sits with his party on one side and one on the other.'

Armstrong shrugged. 'Is it true that the King loses his senses on occasion.'

'Yes, he's had bouts of madness. They try and keep it quiet but gossip is gossip and it leaks out, but he's in his right mind for now, so they say.'

There was so much noise and laughter and shouting across the floor that Armstrong wondered if those on the stage would ever be heard, but then, suddenly, the noise died down and he noticed that members of the orchestra had appeared and were taking their places. The conductor bowed to the audience, the players took up their instruments and a merry tune struck up. The audience hushed and then, before long the huge curtains on the stage were drawn up and the performance began.

It was a piece called 'Something to Do', though in truth, Armstrong could make little sense of it but he enjoyed all the activity. There was singing and dancing and even a pretend sword fight and the setting, largely, it seemed, in a woodland glade, was pleasing. One actress had a very large part and was on stage most of the time, and Armstrong guessed she must be famous but when he asked his companion who she was, he grinned and tapped the side of his nose.

'She's the mistress of the rich man who's funding all this,' he whispered. 'He indulges her though she's not the most talented.'

Armstrong nodded. He was already tiring of her and was looking among the others behind her, trying to spot Sally. At last he saw her, singing and acting her heart out in the chorus.

She should have a larger part. She's a proper actress.

As the play progressed, Armstrong continued to be confused and found it hard to make any sense of the story, but he enjoyed the atmosphere as he quaffed some ale and joined in the laughter and ribaldry at the half time interval.

When the performance was finished and the cast had taken their bows and been booed or clapped, he fought his way through the press of the throng and went round the side of the building to the stage door.

He was not alone. There were plenty of stage door johnnies there hoping to catch the eye of the main actors or of a pretty chorus girl in the hope of persuading her to join them for supper. Armstrong watched in amusement as they were mostly turned down and went sadly on their way and he felt full of pride when, finally, Sally emerged, her eyes a-sparkle and looking pretty as a picture, a bonnet tied under her chin, anchoring her unruly brown curls, and a cloak round her shoulders against the cool of the night. One of the hopefuls approached her but she batted him away, laughing, then she caught sight of Armstrong and came over to him and took hold of his good arm.

'Well, what did you think, Sergeant? Was I right to make you come?'

He smiled down at her. 'Aye,' he said.

And then, of a sudden, he was lost for words. There was much he wanted to say but he was a rough soldier with no practice in giving compliments and never fully at ease in the company of women. He'd always been more comfortable surrounded by men, preferably soldiers, but suddenly all their lewd jokes and talk about women seemed so much boastful nonsense.

Sally was chattering on about the show, what had happened backstage, how it was a shame that the star of the piece could neither sing nor act, and Armstrong found himself just enjoying it all, her talk, her vivacity and, above all, her presence at his side. He was conscious of some jealous looks as they walked on together and he found it impossible to wipe the grin from his face.

'You got any idea where to take me to supper then, Sergeant?'

Armstrong hesitated. 'Well,' he began ..

'Just so long as it's not near Seven Dials,' she said. Then, as he didn't answer for, in truth, the only taverns he knew of were there, she continued. 'Come on then,' she said. 'We'll go to where the theatricals go. It's just round the corner and the victuals aren't bad.'

The tavern was already crowded and they had to push their way in but then Sally spotted Lottie waving at them from a table near the fire and they squeezed in beside her. The fug of smoke made Armstrong's eyes water and the noise of talk and laughter was so loud that he had trouble hearing anything Sally said, giving him an excuse to lean in towards her.

As they were late arrivals, it took a while for their food to arrive – a mixture of cooked meats with oil, some bread and a jug of ale – and, as most others had eaten, gradually the crowd began to disperse.

Armstrong knew he must convey the news of Jack's death to the two girls but he was loathe to spoil the happy atmosphere with tidings of gloom so it wasn't until they, too, were preparing to leave that at last he cleared his throat and told them, as gently as possible, that Jack was dead. He had not had the heart to tell them before, and he had discussed with Will how much he was at liberty to say to them about what happened in France. So, he did not tell them that Jack had been shot by Montagu but simply that he had died in the service of his country.

As he knew it must, the atmosphere changed abruptly.

Sally's hand froze as she was wrapping her cloak around her shoulders. She turned to stare at him, and her eyes began to brim with tears.

'Oh no, not Mr Jack. He was a lovely man. How did it happen?'

'He died serving his country,' said Armstrong.

'But how? Who was the villain that killed him?'

Armstrong reached for her hand and put it to his lips. She did not draw it away but continued to stare at him.

'A traitor, Sal. That's all I can say.'

She withdrew her hand then, rubbing her eyes with the back of her hand and sniffing.

'But you were with Mr Will, so he's safe at least?'

'He is safe. He has to go to inform his family of Jack's death.'

'And what about his poor wife? Does she know?'

'Aye, she will by now. The Captain was on his way to see her when we parted.'

Chapter Nineteen

As the coach travelled North, Will tried to sleep but though he was exhausted, his mind was too full of thoughts of the last few days and he found that he could only doze intermittently and then his dreams were fragmented and frightening, jerking him awake once more.

I wonder if Clara has left yet? Will she go North with her brother, perhaps? Will she tell him that I caused Jack's death? Surely, she would not be so cruel, or so indiscreet? But I know she will never forgive me. She will never look at me again with anything but hatred. She will never again be that girl of my childhood, laughing at me, leaping over fences on her father's horse or teasing Jack. How did I not know that Jack loved her? But then, Jack was good at keeping secrets.

His thoughts drifted back to his childhood, growing up with Jack. Jack who had encouraged him to take up a military life, who had, indeed, persuaded their father to scrape together enough money to buy Will's commission. His father, a hard-working tenant farmer, not some rich aristocrat with land and property of his own. It had been a sacrifice but his parents had been so proud of him. So proud of them both.

Now I am returning to them doubly disgraced and with the news of Jack's death. Can I ever redeem myself?

Then his thoughts turned to the Sergeant. He and Sally had seen him off and wished him God speed. Armstrong had gripped his arm as he boarded the coach.

'You'll serve your country again, sir.'

That remark still rang in his ears and gave him comfort as did the comment from Reeves. 'Jack is someone who I trusted utterly and it seems to me that you are cut from the same cloth.'

So, there are those who still trust me.

***

It was a long and tedious journey but eventually the coach was rolling through the Northumberland countryside with its fields of grazing sheep enclosed by stone walls. Northumberland, where his betrayer's father had recruited his volunteer force to arrest smugglers.

Can I ever prove my innocence? Shall I ever be rid of the shadow cast by that bastard?

At the final stop before his destination, Will went into the coaching inn, took a little refreshment and tried to tidy himself up somewhat. He caught sight of his reflection. A lined face, tousled hair and stained clothes.

Then he remembered something his Colonel had said to him once, long before the incident which had ruined him.

'You are an excellent officer, Fraser. There are too many privileged young men recruited to the army from the grand families of Britain. We need more men like you with a practical head on your shoulders and a love of the men who serve under you.'

That remark had bolstered him at a time when he felt inferior to his fellow officers and he had never forgotten it.

He stood up straight and squared his shoulders.

'And by God,' he muttered to his reflection. 'I swear that I shall make an excellent spy, too.'

Historical Notes

Leaving the Army in disgrace
It was extremely rare for an officer to be cashiered from the military in the 19th century and would only happen following imprisonment and a trial. If found guilty he could be publicly humiliated which could involve a parade-ground ceremony in front of assembled troops with the destruction of his symbols of status. His epaulettes would be ripped off his shoulders, his badges and insignia stripped, his sword broken, his cap knocked away and his medals torn off and dashed to the ground. It also meant that the amount he had paid for his commission was lost, as he could not sell it on.

In this story, I have imagined that Will was accused of insubordination and cowardice. His accuser a well born and jealous officer, who, because of family ties, had considerable influence in Will's regiment. However, Will was saved the humiliation of a trial by the intervention of his Colonel who spoke up for him and persuaded the authorities to give Will the option of resigning from the army without a pension.

Smuggling of Spies and Contraband
Smuggling had always taken place along the South coast of England and it was rife during the Napoleonic wars when contraband was taken both ways across the Channel as were spies and escaped prisoners of war. Hastings had a long tradition of smuggling and many of the fishing families augmented their incomes with smuggling activities. You can visit St Clement's Caves, a large network of caves in Hastings where contraband was concealed.

The Apus of London was a real galley and was intercepted just off the French port of Gravelines by an English gunboat. Gold ingots and coins were found concealed on the crew members and letters to French merchants hidden in the false top of a barrel.

Small paint pots were also discovered, concealed in a secret drawer. These contained black and white paint for the purpose of changing the vessel's name.

In the final years of the Napoleonic wars, Napoleon allowed English smugglers entry into the French ports of Dunkirk and Gravelines, encouraging them to run contraband back and forth across the Channel. Gravelines catered for up to 300 English smugglers housed in a specially constructed compound.

The Alien Office

The Alien Office was the first comprehensive British secret service in the modern sense, and therefore the forerunner of not only the Special Operations Executive (S.O.E.) but also of MI5 and MI6. Although ostensibly part of the Home Office, the wider remit of The Alien Office included the domestic and external surveillance of foreign people of interest. John Reeves was head of the Alien Office from 1803-1814 and had a network of agents who sent information back to their handlers. Messages were often written in code and/or in special inks to try and ensure that their contents would not be revealed should they be intercepted. Each intelligence agency had its own ciphers and ink composition.

Royalist Uprisings

In 1793, during the French Revolution, The Minister of Police, Joseph Fouché, suppressed an insurrection in Lyon against the regime with the utmost savagery. On his return to Paris he is quoted as saying 'The blood of criminals fertilises the soil of liberty and establishes power on sure foundations.' Fouché compiled what we would call a card index, a database of 1,000 active royalists.

In 1795 another insurrection by royalists in Northern France had been planned but had to be aborted after the capture of the royalist agent, Marquis de Bésignan, who had been carrying papers which exposed the identity and activities of many of his fellow agents. At one stroke, this destroyed all that the Alien Office and their associates had been working towards in that area. I have used this real event as the basis for the imagined planned insurrection in this story.

In Britain, Napoleon was vilified in pamphlets and other publications, portrayed as 'The Corsican Demon' and 'The Corsican Monster' and he was blamed for exaggerated atrocities. There were several failed attempts to assassinate him, largely funded by Britain.

The Theatre Royal, Covent Garden

On 20 September 1808, the Theatre Royal, Covent Garden, was destroyed by fire. It was estimated that the loss of property was around £150,000 of which only £50,000 was covered by insurance. To raise sufficient funds to rebuild the theatre, the management issued subscription shares of £500 each. George, Prince of Wales, laid the foundation stone of the new theatre on 31 December 1808, and within ten months, the theatre had been rebuilt.

The Theatre Royal, Drury Lane

Nicknamed 'The King's Playhouse' the Theatre Royal, Drury Lane was destroyed by fire in 1672. A second theatre on the site was demolished and a third burnt down in February 1809, despite it being the first to have a safety curtain. On being encountered drinking a glass of wine in the street while watching the fire, the owner/manager Richard Sheridan was famously reported to have said: "A man may surely be allowed to take a glass of wine by his own fireside."

Travel in the early 19th Century

At the time of this story (1808-9), horse drawn coaches were how people travelled on long journeys, but with the advent of the railways, travelling was transformed. The first train arrived at Hastings station in 1851.

About the Author

After a career as a writer of children's and young adult fiction, Rosemary Hayes now writes historical fiction for adults. Her first book in the genre was *The King's Command,* also published by Sharpe Books, about the terror and tragedy suffered by the French Huguenots during the reign of Louis XIV. Based loosely on the experience of her own Huguenot ancestors, it is a fast-moving story of love and loss. It traces the gradual disintegration of a family who refused to convert to Catholicism, their persecution, their courage and their eventual flight to England in the late 17th century. The book has already collected a couple of awards and some outstanding reviews.

Soldier Spy: Traitor's Game is the first book in a trilogy set during the time of the Napoleonic Wars. The main protagonist is Captain Will Fraser, a disgraced and penniless ex-soldier, the victim of a conspiracy led by a jealous and influential officer. Falsely accused of insubordination and cowardice and dismissed from his regiment, Will is desperate to clear his name. But then his life takes an unexpected turn and he and his injured friend, Sergeant Duncan Armstrong, inadvertently become embroiled in the murky world of spying.

Rosemary's many books for children are written in a variety of different genres, from edgy teenage fiction (*The Mark),* historical fiction (*The Blue Eyed Aborigine* and *Forgotten Footprints),* middle grade fantasy (*Loose Connections, The Stonekeeper's Child* and *Break Out)* to chapter books for early readers and texts for picture books. Many of her books for young people have won or been shortlisted for awards and several have been translated into different languages.

Rosemary has travelled widely but now lives in South Cambridgeshire. She has a background in publishing, having worked for Cambridge University Press before setting up her own company Anglia Young Books which she ran for some years. She has been a reader for a well known authors' advisory service and runs creative writing workshops for both children and adults.

Visit her website at www.rosemaryhayes.co.uk
Find her on **X** (formerly Twitter) @HayesRosemary